PRAISE FOR RIO YOUERS

"*Westlake Soul* is a novel of astonishing beauty and skill. In every generation there are writers who can reveal the souls of the characters that live inside their stories while simultaneously laying bare the secrets of the reader's own heart, if only to them. Rio Youers is such a writer, and *Westlake Soul*—with all its pain, terror, beauty, wonder, and redemption—is such a novel: a classic in the making by an unforgettable, major new voice in speculative fiction."

—Michael Rowe, author of *Enter, Night*

"Rio Youers is one of the reasons why I'm incredibly excited about, and optimistic for, the future of horror fiction. If you haven't read his work before then start right here! *Westlake Soul* is a novel about the very essence of what it is to be human. Numinous, poignant and achingly emotional, it is both deeply tragic and soaringly life-affirming."

—Mark Morris

"There are writers who are so talented that they can make you see the external manifestations of horror in all their full-blown Technicolor ghastliness. And then there are even more talented writers who make you feel horror's heartrending internal effects. Rio Youers falls squarely into the latter category."

—Dark Scribe Magazine

"Rio Youers' storytelling is so charming, so affable, so apparently effortless, that you're still grinning like an idiot when the sheer horror of his imagination leaps up and suckerpunches you in the gut."

—Robert Shearman

WESTLAKE SOUL

RIO YOUERS

ChiZine Publications

FIRST EDITION

Westlake Soul © 2012 by Rio Youers
Cover artwork © 2012 by Erik Mohr
Interior design © 2012 by Samantha Beiko & Danny Evarts
All Rights Reserved.

Library and Archives Canada Cataloguing in Publication

Youers, Rio, 1971-
    Westlake Soul / Rio Youers.

ISBN 978-1-926851-55-6

   I. Title.

PS8647.O58W48 2012   C813'.6   C2011-907418-4

CHIZINE PUBLICATIONS
Toronto, Canada
www.chizinepub.com
info@chizinepub.com

Edited and copyedited by Brett Savory
Proofread by Sandra Kasturi

 Canada Council   Conseil des Arts
for the Arts   du Canada

We acknowledge the support of the Canada Council for the Arts which last year invested $20.1 million in writing and publishing throughout Canada.

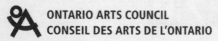 ONTARIO ARTS COUNCIL
CONSEIL DES ARTS DE L'ONTARIO

Published with the generous assistance of the Ontario Arts Council.

For Emily
Ten thousand Fahrenheit

WESTLAKE SOUL

I
ROTTEN APPLE

1. NOT A PIP.

Somebody somewhere is writing this down. This I know; I'm a living (kind of), breathing genius. I'm reaching out and making it happen—from right here: the vegetable patch. Albert Einstein couldn't do that. The dude was shit-hot with atomic bombs and the theory of relativity, but could he talk to dogs? And Goethe . . . nobody used their 10% of the iceberg more effectively, but when it came to tapping the ego and the id, he was just like the rest of you.

My name is Westlake Soul. I know what you're thinking... a name like that I could be one of Gladys Knight's backing singers. One of her Pips. But I'm not a Pip. I'm a twenty-three-year-old former surfing champion (Billabong Classic '07, Ride the Barrel '08). I live in Hallow Falls, Ontario, with my parents, my little sister, and our dog, Hub. You want a description? Imagine Stephen Hawking. Now lose the glasses and give him a Kurt Cobain haircut. It's pretty close.

I'm smarter than Hawking, though. Like, *much*. He's too chickenshit to take an IQ test, but I can tell you he'd register in the 160s. Me? Dude, I'd break the gauge. The

Wechsler Adult Intelligence Scale was not designed for a mind like mine. It'd be like a weathervane in a tornado. A thermometer on the sun.

All superheroes get their powers from somewhere. A radioactive spider bite. A science experiment gone awry. I got mine from a surfing accident in Tofino. The ultimate wipeout. I woke up with the most powerful mind on the planet, but a body like a wet paper bag. I'm not cool with the trade-off, but such is life.

I won't be like this for long, though . . . being fed through a tube, my mouth hanging open, fucking drooling. I'm going to use my superbrain to drag myself from this (permanent) vegetative state.

You can forget saving the world.

I just want to surf again.

2. RELEASE.

The ocean is 621.2 kilometres away, but I can see it whenever I want. All I have to do is project my soul, which is easy without the distractions of the conscious mind. Imagine holding a feather in front of an electric fan and then letting go. If your focus is the feather, or the breeze from the fan, then you fail. If your focus is the *letting go*—the precise moment of release—then give yourself a gold star.

I'm going to show you so much cool stuff.

Come with me. . . .

Rolling blue sea and spray that shimmers like a smile. That embracing ocean smell, the chorus of breaking waves, and gulls curving their wings into the thermals. A catamaran skims along the blue, its sail full of life, and farther out—*miles*, I can reach as far I want—a humpback breaches, its scarred, muscular body twisting through the air. Weave yourself around its dorsal ridges and ride with me. Feel it. Be it. You are not a person, a gas, or a light. You are that moment of release, attached to life. The water rushes through you and the whale's body sings. You spiral and descend. Its heartbeat makes you glow.

What else am I going to do? Look at the frickin' ceiling? Roll my head, look at the frickin' wall?

Please.

Okay, that's not entirely fair. My parents have done their best to make my room cool and comfortable. *Pretty groovy*, Mom said once they'd finished decorating. I wouldn't go that far. I can't imagine Earth, Wind & Fire wanting to hang out here for very long. The décor is designed to be stimulating. There's a lot of happy colour. A shade of yellow from Benjamin Moore called Little Angels. The ceiling painted Surf City Blue. There's an egg chair in the corner like the one Mork sat in when calling Orson. Couple of bean bags. Pictures of me on the wall, surfing, playing hockey, meeting Patrick Swayze. A window looking out on the back garden. Shelves loaded with my surfing trophies. A yucca in another corner that mocks me with its healthy leaves.

I don't mean to be cynical. I'm truly grateful for all the love and care I receive, but I know for a fact that the groovy makeover was more for my parents' benefit than mine. They told themselves that the colours and trophies could help "wake" me, but didn't believe it for one second. They—fuck, *everybody*, except Hub—has this crazy idea that because I don't respond to stimuli, I feel no pain or emotion. So why bother painting the ceiling blue or hanging pictures of me catching barrels? Shit, you don't need a superbrain to answer that question. They did it because I'm depressing to be around. Heartbreaking, even. It's no fun wiping spit off my chin and listening to me grunt. The colours lift the mood. It's as simple as that.

I have a wheelchair, too. It has buffers to keep my head from flopping around too much. From gutterballing—

that's what Dad calls it. Most days I'm rolled out to the living room. Just for an hour or so, then I'm back in my brightly painted box. If the weather is nice I'll be wheeled onto the rear deck. I'm not sure why, given they believe me insensible. Actually, I *am* sure why. It's to assuage their guilt. They don't feel so bad about having a good time if I'm sitting in the fresh air with too much sunscreen on my arms. Again, I know that sounds cynical, but that's just the way it is.

One day last summer, they were having *such* a good time that they forgot about me—left me on the goddamn deck for most of the night. Dad got trashed on cheap beer, and Mom had been at the Crown Royal. They were in the living room watching shit TV, and my sister was in her bedroom showing her titties on Skype. I waited . . . *waited*. My sister flicked off the webcam and got into bed with her iPod cranking Lil Wayne. Mom got frisky and dragged Dad into the bedroom. Now I'm faced with a dilemma: do I wait and see if they'll suddenly remember that they've left me on the deck, or do I try to send a telepathic memorandum? I didn't hold out much hope for either; I'm not so hot at the whole Professor X thing—you know, controlling their minds (not one of my superpowers), and although I can jump into their heads whenever I want, it isn't something I like to do. Their thoughts are too close, too personal. You ever had your mom or dad talk to you about sex? *Their* sex, I mean. *We used to have to do it in the back of your father's Catalina.* Or, *Your mother was a saucy little minx back in the day.* Ewww, right? Don't go there, right? Yeah, it's like that, but a thousand times worse.

So I woke Hub. I told him to start barking like Lassie,

or something. Hub did. He even scratched on my parents' bedroom door. But all he got for his trouble was my old man's foot up his ass.

That didn't go as planned, Hub said to me.

The mosquitoes were in full force at this point. I even had a few in my mouth. So I reached out and knocked on Dad's mind. Real quick, then ran away before I could see what he was thinking. Dad's humping Mom by now, pulling a stupid face, sweat in his beard. Then he just kind of stopped mid-stroke.

"What is it?" Mom asked.

"Not sure," Dad said, his eyes all glassy.

"Did you come already?"

"No . . . did you turn off the stove?"

"What?"

"Never mind," Dad said, and carried on humping.

I was pretty pissed off, as you can imagine. Not because I'd been left outside and the mosquitoes were partying like it was Mardi-fucking-Gras, but because I'd been *forgotten*. And suddenly I didn't want them to remember me. I wanted them to wake up in the morning and find me with dew on my eyelids and a caterpillar in my mouth—to feel a tidal wave of guilt, for it to crush them and pull them under, and leave them feeling like shit for weeks. No less than they deserved. Hub asked if he should try barking again. *No,* I said. *Fuck 'em*. And I released . . . flew away. I went to the ocean and swam with dolphins in the moonlight.

Anyway, Hub *did* start barking again. He told me it was because he needed a night-piss, but I didn't believe him. Dude was looking out for me. Dad cursed and got out of bed, let Hub out, then noticed me sitting on the deck.

"Oh, fuck Jesus," he said. "Jesus fuck." He wheeled me back inside. "Sorry, Wes. We just . . ."

Yeah. You forgot. I know. Asshole.

They've only forgotten me once. But there was another embarrassing outdoors moment. I was sitting on the deck, pondering the simplicity of the Riemann hypothesis (like you do), when a bird landed on my head. A goldfinch, too. The most arrogant of birds.

What the fuck is going on? I said. *Excuse me . . . bird . . . you mind?*

The finch shook its yellow feathers. *Relax, dude*, it said. *I'm just taking five. I've been flying all day, so don't give me your jive.*

Outwardly I had no reaction, but inwardly I was agape.

I'm sorry, I said. *Did you just . . . rhyme to me?*

There's a whole world of difference between rhyming and song. I thought you were smart, but I guess I was wrong.

Let's not discuss the fundamentals of verse, I said. *Get the hell off my head.*

Niki, my sister (it's short for Phereniki—my parents truly are fucked in the head), came outside then, yapping on her cell phone, trying to sound American even though she's from small-town Ontario.

"So I'm, like, *really?*" she yapped, rolling her eyes. "And he's, like, *really?*" She glanced at me, then pulled one of those comical double takes.

"Ohmygod," she said. One word. The thought balloon in her mind read, OMG. Then it read, LMFAO as she started to laugh her fucking ass off. "Westlake has, like, *totally* got a bird on his head."

And I'm, like, *really?*

"I'm not kidding," she said. "I'll take a picture and *totally* e-mail it to you."

So she took a picture and totally e-mailed it to her friend. Then she took another and totally uploaded it to her Facebook page.

"Mom-Dad," she shouted. "Come quick. Westlake has got a bird on his head."

So Mom and Dad came outside and they started laughing, too.

Satisfied? I asked the finch.

Stop being so square, the finch replied. *Stop being so bitter. It's been a long time since you gave them a titter.*

"Does that have video?" Dad asked, pointing at Niki's cell phone.

"Hell yeah," she replied, and started recording.

"Priceless," Dad said.

Mom slapped Dad's shoulder playfully, wiped tears from her eyes, then did the decent thing and shooed the bird away.

Go on, Tweety Pie, I said. *Fuck out of here.*

It took wing in a brief tick of yellow, cussing me in rhyme, like an R-rated, avian version of Dr. Seuss.

No wonder I release. I'm trapped in body, but not in mind—in soul. It feels like a horse behind a starting gate, pushing and frothing, and all I have to do is throw the gate open. The horse bolts. There's no stopping it. To the ocean. To the mountains. Wherever. It's wild, powerful and fast.

I don't always release to exotic locales. Sometimes I'll hang with my old buddies while they cruise Hallow Falls or go clubbing, although that makes me sad because I'm not physically with them. And despite my family being a lovable pain in the ass, I'll often float into the next room . . . sit with Dad while he illegally downloads music or plays *World of Warcraft*. Or I'll watch Mom reading or watering the plants. She sings to them, softly, and I like that.

But what I like more is the fact that they're being natural. There is no false hope. They're in a place where they're not thinking about me—where they don't *have* to think about me, and that's exactly how I like to see them. It warms my heart. It's so beautiful.

The ocean, though. The world's emotion. Sometimes calm. Sometimes raging. Always deep. Where it began—life on earth. Where it will end. And I go there, when the box just isn't bright enough. I throw myself into its moiling depths and remember what it was like to ride. To feel the life beneath my board. Aquamarine in my lungs. Salt in my hair. The top of a wave curling over me, gathering me, like God's wing.

3. How to Make a Superhero.

Perfection is clear in my mind. The birdlike weight of her hand in mine. Her breath so sweet, almost toffee. The way her lips danced across my skin, and the wishes in her eyes—my wishes, yet to be granted.

Nadia Charles. Name like a Bond girl. She looked like a Bond girl, too, with a swirl of black hair and a body so precise you'd think she'd been designed. Suspicious beauty. I have all my memories of her, and they're vivid enough to relive at any time (a benefit of reclining in what Jung called the personal unconscious, and what I call secondhand reality). My favourite memory is the one that hurts the most. Our last morning together. The last time we made love. The last time we kissed.

I relive it often; pain helps me feel normal.

"Baby," she had said. "Open the blinds a little. I love pink sunshine."

We were on vacation in Tofino, British Columbia. Three weeks of beach life. Me, my best friend Darryl, and our girls. Surfing all day. Kick-ass parties by night. The roar of the Pacific. Beer bottles popping open. The kind of music that makes everyone dance. It was supposed to be the best summer ever. The one we'd remember until we could remember no more.

Early morning, touching dawn. Nadia had just woken up. Her dark eyes had that crinkled, sleepy look. Adorable. I cracked the blinds and diagonals of pink light jumped into our room. They touched her body like lines on a stave. I kissed her. Random notes, like a cat walking across piano keys.

"Here," she said, and opened herself for me.

A thousand clichés. She made me feel alive. She was the ocean. Time stood still. All I ever wanted. The truth is, all were relevant. But there was more—the little things that prosaisms could never relate. The way our teeth would sometimes clash when we kissed. Our similar laugh. That we were always first on the dance floor. How she insisted on unzipping my wetsuit because she liked to see the tight material separate, my toned traps revealed. Ad infinitum . . . the things that defined us.

"I want to be your Soul," she said after we had made love for the final time.

"Nadia Soul?" I asked.

"I like how that sounds," she said.

I smiled and ran my finger down the middle of her body, from the hollow of her throat to the place where her pubic hair was beginning to grow back in. I left a trail in our sweat that caught the pink light like a strip of chrome.

"I like how that sounds, too," I said.

She was nineteen. I was twenty-one. We'd met the previous summer at the Skate-Krazy tourney in Toronto.

I wouldn't say it was love at first sight, but Nadia was definitely *cool* at first sight. The kind of girl that makes your ego purr. She was deejaying the men's vert prelims, Allen & Heath headphones parked on one ear, responding to crowd noise with insane effects and backspins. She was wearing a white bikini top and a jean skirt. Donna Karan shades. The Rip Curl logo for a tramp stamp. My kind of girl.

I approached her at the after-party. She was with some thug called Farley. Think of the guy at your local gym who spends thirty seconds on power reps, then ten minutes strutting, flexing, checking himself out in every mirror. Yeah, that's Farley. I didn't need to introduce myself; Nadia knew who I was. We were Facebook friends, apparently. Farley shook my hand and squeezed too hard. I gave him a smile to let him know that everything was chill, even though I had every intention of SuperPoking his girlfriend.

I threw a sheep at her. She threw a chicken at me. I chest-bumped her. She high-fived me. I tickled her. She blew a kiss at me.

Farley saw this interaction, of course. He responded with a SuperPoke of his own. He roundhouse kicked me. I snapped his bra. He dropkicked me. I threw a ShamWow at him.

A private message from Farley. Nothing in the subject line. Just a badly spelled warning: *Beter watch yur step you fuckin ass clown.*

I unfriended and blocked him, but not before throwing a ninja star his way. Then I sent a private message to Nadia: *I upset your boyfriend. Guess he doesn't like me poking you.* She sent one back: *He's not my boyfriend, exactly. Just a dude who wants to be. And I like when you poke me. Don't stop.*

The rest happened quickly, effortlessly. Thirteen months of loving that began with a thrown sheep, and ended in pink sunshine. Of course, I had no idea it was the end. I thought we were still at the beginning.

In our final moments of togetherness, I drew stars around Nadia's nipples and thought how incredible her skin smelled, and how the sun had coloured it perfectly. She was imagining (I didn't know this then, but do now) our wedding. Somewhere hot. On the beach. She was dressed in a white sarong, an orchid in her hair. I was dressed in a Rastafarian tam, Bermuda shorts, and espadrilles. Our page boy had coffee skin and dreadlocks. The service was conducted by the Reverend Al Green.

"Are you going out?" she asked me.

I heard the ocean, calling to me.

"Yeah," I said.

"It's still early," she said.

"The best time," I said. "No kooks in my way. I should catch some good rollers."

She touched my chest. "You can stay here. Roll with me."

This was the moment. When I recall everything that happened, this moment sits heaviest on my soul. It is Y-shaped, bound in chains that rattle, *if only . . . if only*, with a near-human voice. How different would my life be if I had stayed with Nadia and let the waves roll alone? This isn't the time to discuss quantum mechanics, but consider, for one second, the relative state formulation—a universal wave function that doesn't collapse at each branch point, and implies the existence of parallel worlds. According to this theory, there are infinite Westlake Souls out there, living in infinite dimensions, each one splitting into the next. In one of these worlds I stayed with Nadia in the pink sunshine. We made love again, and again. I didn't go surfing, and subsequently didn't drown in the ocean. There's a Westlake Soul out there who *did* marry Nadia on a beach in the Caribbean . . . but in the reality I know the wave function collapses.

I kissed Nadia for the last time and went surfing.

If only.

I have, incidentally, sought these parallel worlds, to the point where my brilliant mind aches with the effort. If I could access that critical branch point, I could live an alternate life with no knowledge of this one. I'd have my body back. My girl. Failure to come close throws into question Hugh Everett III's relative state formulation. Either the theory is nonsense or the universal wave function cannot be accessed on a psychic level, which makes it impossible to prove.

In other words . . . I'm stuck with this life.

With that last kiss still on my lips I strolled down to the beach, my board under one arm, my bag slung over one shoulder. The waves were primo, climbing high and breaking hard. There was a guy throwing a Frisbee for his dog to catch, but otherwise the beach was mine. I set down my board and applied a layer of wax, my eyes never leaving the ocean. A rippling blue/white flag that I couldn't wait to fly. I got a read on the waves and decided to switch to a 10mm leash. More drag, but less likely to break in the heavies. Another critical branch point. If I had stuck with the 5mm, maybe the leash would have broken, taking the board away from me, rather than having it boomerang and crack me in the skull. So many ifs, and all insignificant.

I stepped out, now living the last thirty-two minutes of life as I knew it. I remember feeling the sand push between my toes, and the surf fizzing around my ankles. Sensations I have always loved. The dog barked happily as I moved into deeper water, then paddled out to the action. The first wave I caught surprised me. It was fast and rough, but I tamed it with my balance, attacking the lip and reentering to let it know who was boss. I rode it backhand until it was spent. The second wave was a cruncher and I wiped out as soon as I got to my feet. The ocean laughed and pulled at me but I grabbed the rails of my board and popped back up. I schooled it with the next set, hitting cutbacks and aerials, then shooting the curl and howling with exhilaration. Nothing comes close to this feeling. Not for me, at least. Maybe snowboarding an avalanche, or skateboarding an earthquake. I cry inside. Jubilant, exultant tears. I'm quite literally riding the world, and that's exactly how it feels. If making love to a beautiful person is heaven, then surfing is God.

I laughed—it was the last time I ever laughed—and paddled out to the heavies again. And then I saw it. A wall of water surging toward me, filling the horizon. A no-nonsense, freakish motherfucker of a wave, its sole purpose to prove how small and inconsequential I was. My instinct screamed to back down but I was charged inside and nothing could stop me. The rest of the world disappeared. I felt both tiny and limitless.

This was my every wish. My every nightmare.

This was the wave that would kill me.

I caught it perfectly, rising up the face, springing to my feet and feeling the push behind the board. I was ready for the speed, but not the power—thought I was, but it sucked the air from my lungs and drove me into the trough so hard that I almost lost it. Fists pummelled on the bottom of my board and the spray was like teeth. I refused to bail, though, even when I could hear the white water behind me, a thunderhead of sound, bigger than the moon. I turned into the open face and locked in. No chance of pulling any tricks. It was all I could do to keep from getting nailed. Then came the moment I lived for (ironically, the moment I died for): the lip of the wave curling over me, surging ahead of me, and all at once I was riding through a perfect cylinder of water. The barrel. The glasshouse. The green room. A surreal and powerful experience. As close to dreaming as you can get while still awake. I clenched my fists and roared.

There was a tiny circle of daylight at the end of the barrel, filled with spray and tangerine sky. I aimed for it, but the wave was closing around me fast. No way I would make it in time. I considered pulling out, fractionally shifting my back foot, and this was all the hesitation the wave needed. It lifted the tail of my board and threw me. I was airborne for less than a second, then chewed up and swallowed. The power was otherworldly. I had challenged thousands of waves and many of them had gotten the better of me, but I had never known anything like this. An atom bomb in the ocean. An aquatic black hole. My body was thrown down, dragged up, tossed around. Just another piece of seaweed about to be cast limply on the shore. I tried to protect myself—to curl into a ball and cover my head with both hands—but I had no control over my body. I was pushed deep, dragged along the sandy floor, skin sheared from my face and hands. My heart thrashed and my lungs ached for air. Pale thoughts opened in my mind, and as I was sucked up for another go-round, my board whipped on its leash, cut through the water like a ray, and slammed me in the middle of my forehead.

I saw Nadia in that moment, lying on our bed with the ruffled sheet clutched between her legs, between her breasts. A leaf of hair pressed against her left cheek, curled at the tip. The light, through the blinds, was wilder. She blinked her huge eyes, like a woodland animal in a Disney cartoon, and I screamed for her. I didn't want this wave anymore. This ocean. I wanted my beautiful girlfriend, to fall into her body as I had less than an hour before, draw star-shapes around her nipples and ride deep inside her. I called her name but there was no sound. Not even a shimmer in the air. My hand, reaching for her, was imagined. The depression my head had made in the pillow was still there. It was like my ghost—as close to her as I could get.

Jimi's guitar, loud and raw. "Little Wing" flowed from the radio in Darryl's room. I flowed, too, away from Nadia, passing through two walls to see Darryl with his girl, her legs hooked onto his shoulders, both of them gasping, sweating, sounds of passion enveloped by the music. This is what my best friend was doing while I drowned in the ocean. You'd think there'd be some sense of foreboding. A prescience. Nothing radical, just a pause in what he was doing—a *funny feeling* that something was wrong. I'd known him for sixteen years, after all. But no, he was oblivious, far too preoccupied with getting down on it, like Kool & the Gang. He couldn't hear me—couldn't *feel* me— no matter how loud I screamed.

I backflipped out of there and floated in a cold band of sky over Vancouver Island, listening to Jimi play as my body died. I'm sure you've read accounts of people who have gone through near-death experiences. The inner peace. The bright light. It's not like that—it's fucking terrifying. I wanted only to shuffle back into my body and resurface in the ocean, with nothing more serious than a headache and a dented ego. I screamed but nobody heard me. I reached out but touched nothing. The island lay beneath me, shaped like a broken wing. I could see the fierce push of the ocean and a brushstroke of sand. But it wasn't mine anymore. Whatever had been holding me to the earth had snapped and I was floating away . . . into a sky that was painfully blue, toward a sun that looked more like a howling face.

Outside: my body was dragged onto the shore by the man who'd been throwing the Frisbee. His dog ran around me, wild circles, the Frisbee clamped in her jaws. The man administered CPR, but by the time he got my heart started my brain had been starved of oxygen for eight minutes, forty-four seconds.

Inside: I duelled with him, then, for the first time. The first of many. My archenemy. Every superhero has one. Batman has the Joker. Superman has Lex Luthor. Spider-Man has the Green Goblin. Me . . . I have the emperor of darkness.

I have Dr. Quietus.

4. ARCHENEMY.

I am often referred to as a cabbage. A hurtful expression. I've also been called brain-dead on occasion. Equally hurtful, and entirely inaccurate. Okay, so my brain cells started to go kamikaze after five minutes without oxygen, resulting in severe and (apparently) irreversible atrophy of the cerebral cortex. My neurologist, Dr. (I shit you not) Thinker (funny, eh?), MD, FRCPC, PhD, told Mom and Dad that my brain is like a rotten apple. The core—my brain stem—is intact and functioning normally. Hence, I have regular sleep-wake cycles, can circulate blood, manage my secretions (no need for a tracheostomy—thank Christ for small favours), and respire without aid. I'm also capable of random, involuntary movement. The remainder of the "apple" is mushy and brown. It has shrivelled in my skull. Pockets of fluid have replaced lost brain mass. Not an apple you would like to eat, as Dr. Thinker told my parents. Good for nothing, in fact. Dad (bless him; he was overwhelmed with emotion at the time, and trying to make the best out of a bad situation) asked if it was good enough to make apple pie. Dr. Thinker frowned and said no. Mom asked if it was good enough to make cider. "What kind of cider?" Dr. Thinker enquired, clearly confounded by my parents' line of questioning, and Mom (bless her, too) said, "The sweet kind."

Brain damaged? Shit, yeah. Brain fucked? Okay ... sure, if you like. But brain-*dead*? No way, dude. Not even close.

I was in a coma for thirty-seven days. Darkness all the way. An epic battle with Dr. Quietus. I finally woke (insomuch as I opened my eyes) to a chrome-bright hospital room and two weeping parents. The way Mom clutched my hand, the timbre of her sobs, told me that something was very wrong. The cardiac monitor, IV lines, and nasogastric feeding tube reinforced the knowledge. I tried to move my head, but couldn't. I tried to speak—tell Mom not to cry— but couldn't. The severity of my condition dawned like a crippled sun. The smell of flowers was sickening.

"Westlake?" Mom squeezed my hand harder. My knuckles popped. I felt the curve of her wedding ring. The tip of her fingernail. "Baby, can you hear me?"

Yeah, Mom, I said. *I can hear you.*

Imagine something perfect. A flower. A leaf. A work of art. No—nothing material. That's too clichéd. It needs to be a feeling. A perfect feeling. When you see a loved one after a long absence, or recall the sweetest moment of your life with such intense clarity it's like you are living it again. A feeling that, if you could see it, it would sparkle. Pour it into a bottle and it would glow. Now imagine, at its brightest point, this feeling stripped away and replaced with a cold, grave-like hole. This may help you understand how I felt at that moment. The contrast—from flight to fallen, from heaven to hell—was debilitating, suffocating.

"Blink if you can hear me, baby," Mom said.

I couldn't.

Over the next few weeks, while my physical body was subjected to numerous tests and scans and my parents kept their vigil at my bedside, I became aware of my new superhero abilities. It wasn't exactly triumphant. I didn't tear open my shirt to reveal a dazzling "W" or dive into a telephone booth to don my cape and boots. I actually thought I was dreaming. Or hallucinating. A side effect of the fluids they were pumping into me. Understandable, given that I could suddenly comprehend what the birds were singing about, and could think in five thousand different languages. It was easy to shake my soul free while listening to the purr and buzz of the CT scanner, or suffering my mother's sobs. I would fly above the clouds in emotional circles, and alight on top of neo-Gothic skyscrapers. After realizing I wasn't dreaming or hallucinating, I surmised that my mind had engaged some kind of defence mechanism. A way to ease the trauma.

Meanwhile, my parents waited for me to emerge from my vegetative state, praying with clenched hands and bleach-pale fingers. They knew that time was critical, and that my chances of recovery faded with every passing day. Mom would say things like, *Move your head if you can hear me, Westlake*. Or, *Smile if you understand*. And sometimes I would make a random, reflex movement. Maybe I would moan, or twitch—not in response to Mom, but because my autonomic nervous system happened to throw a switch at that moment, giving an impression of awareness. This fuelled my parents' hope, even though Dr. Thinker explained that my "responses" were involuntary, coincidental. But a person in distress will cling to anything, and my parents never stopped believing that I would pull through.

Four weeks after emerging from my coma, my condition was changed to "Persistent Vegetative State." This was when Dr. Thinker likened my brain to a rotten apple. He showed Mom and Dad my CT scan images, pointing out the dark pockets of fluid—the mushy fruit. After assuring them that my brain wasn't good enough for pie or cider (not even the sweet kind), he told them that I had zero chance of making a full recovery, and that I would be a vegetable (at least he didn't call me a cabbage) for the rest of my life.

"I don't believe that," Mom said to Dr. Thinker. "My baby is still in there. I can see him. I can feel him."

I had by this time accepted and embraced my superhero skills, and when I wasn't fighting Dr. Quietus or residing in some blissful secondhand reality, I was seeking a way out. A way to live again. I used all of my strength to channel the motor cortex, trying to scrunch my toes or twitch my fingers, but always without success. Jesus, I was faster than a speeding bullet, more powerful than a locomotive, yet I couldn't wiggle my pinky. I grabbed my board and surfed the universal wave function, thinking I could turn a trick, cut back, and open my eyes to an alternate reality. But the water was glassy and I didn't so much surf as sink, leading me to conclude that life exists only in the present. The past is a rotten apple. Good for nothing. Not even pie.

I screamed at my body to move. At my eyes to open. At my voice to be heard. I hoisted vehicles above my head, smashed through concrete walls, and flew against the earth's rotation fifty thousand times. Nothing. Not a flicker. Exhausted and bereft, I would forsake my useless shell and glide the ocean, listening to its heartbeat as my tears joined the swell.

Trust me, even your soul can cry.

"You should know," Dr. Thinker told my parents, "that Westlake will have no quality of life, and that the burden on you, his parents, will be demanding."

"He's our son," Dad said. "He'll never be a burden."

"There are programmes to help you cope," Dr. Thinker said. "I'll provide you with the relevant information. You should also consider home nursing."

"Whatever it takes," Dad said.

Dr. Thinker nodded. "Also, I should warn you that Westlake's life expectancy is uncertain. He's not as strong as he used to be, and therefore susceptible to infection. He could also develop pneumonia, respiratory problems, or may simply decide to just . . . give up."

Give up? Never. Not as long as there are waves to surf.

"Are you saying," Mom said, "that he could die at any moment?"

"He may live another forty years in his condition," Dr. Thinker replied. "I'm just preparing you for the worst."

"He's a fighter," Mom said.

"Westlake has no cognitive ability whatsoever," Dr. Thinker said. "He's not fighting, Mrs. Soul, because he isn't aware he's in a fight. He isn't aware of *anything*."

Obviously not true. I rapped on Dr. Thinker's mind to tell him as much, but you'd be surprised how quickly rational people dismiss strange voices in their head. It's one of the (many) reasons why communicating with humans on a telepathic level is so difficult, even for me.

He was right about my life expectancy, though. I battle Dr. Quietus frequently. Usually brief, violent confrontations. He comes in many forms, but always sleek and dark. I have never seen his true face. He just slides his cold hands around me. The ultimate supervillain. I need all my mental strength to shake him off. There's a certain ironic humour to the fact that I appear so expressionless on the outside, while inside I'm wrestling my wicked archenemy on top of a cable car in Switzerland, or avoiding his death ray while flying around Tokyo's flickering skyline.

Of all our battles, the first—while my physical body lay comatose—was the longest and most brutal. He came at me, cold and hooded, and filled me with a terror so huge it felt like my soul had been dipped in tar and smashed with a hammer. Cat and mouse to begin with. Son of a bitch could have taken me out whenever he wanted. Instead he cackled and pawed at me. I crawled into a corner and prayed for light. It would have been easier to succumb— maybe manage a couple of hopeless flips, like a fish out of water—but Mom was right: I'm a fighter. I raged against him. We spilled through the streets of my coma, entangled, trading vicious blows. And somewhere in that vastness I discovered my inner strength. Dr. Quietus was no match. He retreated, vowing to return, and I opened my eyes to that chrome-bright room and the deep tone of grief.

Still alive.

But he's there . . . always there. Poised to strike.

My archenemy.

Prior to my return home (to the brightly painted box and Mork egg chair), I astral projected into a meeting between my parents and Dr. Thinker. I wish I hadn't. It was morose . . . worrying. I had been in hospital seven months at this point, and my parents had accepted the probability that my condition would not improve.

"I'm sure you appreciate," Dr. Thinker said, "how demanding Westlake's constant care will be."

Mom and Dad nodded. I drifted around them, lighter than breath. Dad was picking at his cuticles. A nervous habit. Mom was biting her upper lip. Dr. Thinker's thick spectacles reflected the sunlight splashing through the window. His pale eyes were lost in the glare.

"Which leads me to a sensitive issue," he continued. "You may—almost certainly *will*—reach a stage when you seriously contemplate Westlake's quality of life. Or lack of, to be precise. Taking everything into consideration, you may decide that discontinuing life support is the most sympathetic course of action."

Mom's eyes popped open. "You mean killing him?"

"I wouldn't put it that way, Mrs. Soul."

"But ending his life?"

"Discontinuing life support."

"Yes. Ending his life."

Dr. Thinker sat back in his chair and the sunlight bounced off his glasses. I could see his eyes now. Small and gold, with flecks of red. Made me think of the Devil. He plucked his ear lobes—perhaps his own nervous habit—and picked up a pen on his desk. Didn't write with it. Ran his thumb along the barrel.

"I'm not a counsellor, and I'm not here to tell you what's right for you and your son." He tried a compassionate expression, but couldn't nail it. Maybe because of the red flecks in his eyes. "That's a decision only you can make, but experience has taught me that, at some point, you'll ask yourself what Westlake would want. I'm informing you of your options. Nothing more."

Dad nodded and Mom's eyes filled with tears. I flitted, agitated. The shimmer from a candle.

"I can't imagine how difficult this is for you."

Mom fished a Kleenex from her purse and dabbed her cheeks.

"Excuse my ignorance," Dad said. "This is all very surreal and emotional . . . but how would you end life support?"

"His feeding tube would be removed," Dr. Thinker replied.

"Right. Of course." Dad thought about this for a moment. His eyes narrowed. "So he would starve to death?"

"Well, he wouldn't receive the hydration and nutrients required to sustain life."

"Don't pretty it up, Doc. He would starve to death." Dad shook his head. "Jesus Christ, it's not like flicking a switch, is it? How long would he take to die?"

"Impossible to say." Dr. Thinker moved back into the sunlight. His eyes disappeared. "There are many variables. It can take days, sometimes even weeks, depending on hydration levels in the patient."

"*Weeks*?" Dad said. His voice climbed in pitch. He sounds like Mickey Mouse when he gets excited. Mom sometimes finds it hard to keep a straight face when they're arguing. "What are we talking . . . two weeks? Three?"

"In some cases, yes, but again there are many variables."

"And I'm sorry . . . did you use the word *sympathetic*?"

"It's a decision you'll make based on how you feel after

a given period of time, and what you believe Westlake would want."

"I'm pretty sure he wouldn't want to starve to death."

"If he were able to think for himself, do you think he would prefer to remain in a vegetative state for the rest of his life?"

Dad picked at his cuticles and puffed out his cheeks. Mom ruined another Kleenex. There were tiny white shreds in her lap. Down the front of her sweater. Still the tears came. They glowed in the sunlight like Dr. Thinker's spectacles. I continued to flit around the room, amazed that this conversation was even taking place, and wondering if—when I ghosted back into my physical body—I would be trembling.

"And there's no quicker way?" Dad asked.

"Cedar," Mom said. "We're not—"

"I'm only asking," Dad said.

"Quicker?" Dr. Thinker said. "What do you mean?"

"A pill. An injection."

"Cedar—"

"Euthanasia is illegal in Canada, Mr. Soul."

"So inducing a quick, merciful death is illegal," Dad said. "But allowing someone to starve for an indeterminate amount of time is perfectly acceptable?"

"I don't make the rules, Mr. Soul." I could tell from his clipped tone that Dr. Thinker was growing impatient. There were spots of colour on his cheeks as red as the flecks in his eyes. "I'm providing information so that you can make an informed decision should the situation arise."

Thick silence hit the room. It was like blue sky without sunshine. A washed and chilling emptiness. It was broken by Mom, trying not to sob. She hissed, shoulders bobbing, fragments of Kleenex glued to her face by tears.

"Never," she whispered.

I went to her and held her but knew she couldn't feel me.

5. Hub.

His full name is Hubba-Hubba Artful Soul (my parents again, man—I swear to God). He's a schnoodle, a cross between a schnauzer and a poodle, which means he's insufferably cute. Golden fur, drops of black liquid for eyes, a warm nose. Now that I don't see too much of Darryl, or any of the guys, I'd say that Hub is my best friend in the whole world. No, that's wrong; Hub has *always* been my best friend in the whole world. It just took a change in circumstances for me to realize that.

Schnoodles (but don't call him a schnoodle—dude answers to Hub or nothing) are by nature quite active. They love to play. Fetch sticks. Go for walks. Join in when humans are playing Twister. You know the kind—running around, ears cocked, wanting to get involved. But not Hub. It's not that he's lazy. He's just . . . laid back. What can I say? The dude is cool.

We got him from a shelter four years ago. He was eight months old at the time. An unwanted Christmas present. Talk of a family dog had been circulating for a while. Lectures in care and ownership. Name suggestions. Breed suggestions. Feeding and walking schedules. Finally Dad declared us ready and we arrived at the shelter as a family, united, but with completely different ideas about the kind of dog we would be leaving with. Dad wanted something dependable and protective, preferably the size of a horse. Mom wanted something with pleasant breath, and that didn't shed. Niki—going through her Paris Hilton phase— wanted something she could smuggle out of the house in her purse, and that would totally rock a Lady B. Couture dress. I wanted something I could teach how to surf.

To paraphrase Messrs. Jagger and Richards, none of us got what we wanted, but we all got what we needed.

Hubba-Hubba.

Most of the dogs went nuts when we walked into the room, yapping in their cages, pawing at the bars, chasing their tails, fighting for attention. Mom covered her ears while Niki squealed and looked for something suitably purse-sized. Dad rolled his eyes and took a step backward. I could see second thoughts dashing across his face like spooked cattle. One of the few dogs that wasn't barking— wasn't doing anything, in fact—caught my eye. He was lying at the back of his cage, one foreleg covering his eyes, like a man with a headache. I strolled over, crouched, looked through the bars.

"Hey, pooch."

Nothing. Only his pink belly moving as he breathed.

I tapped the bars. He lowered his foreleg and cracked open one eye. This made me laugh. Ever see a dog open just one eye? Doesn't happen very often. He regarded me for a moment, then closed his eye. The foreleg crept back into position.

"I think this dog is hungover," I said. "I want him."

Mom and Dad joined me. I willed the pooch to do something—anything—to endear himself to them, but he remained in the same position, as if he'd just returned from a weekend in Amsterdam.

The attendant gave us the skinny. Unwanted Christmas present. Schnauzer/poodle mix—a schnoodle, by God. Faithful, intelligent, doesn't shed. Mom was sold. I think Dad was sold on the word, "schnoodle." Niki wasn't thrilled, but was outvoted 3-1. She sulked all the way home, texting her friends. I read one of them over her shoulder: FAMILY R RETARDS!! H8 MY LIFE!!! H8 NEW DOG 2!!!

Didn't take long to change her tune, though. Less than two hours later, Hub (though still without a name at this point—Mom and Dad were arguing about it) leapt onto the sofa beside Niki and fell asleep with his head resting in her lap. Niki beamed, braces glimmering, as if Kanye West had curled up next to her and assumed the same position.

"He. Is. Adorable," she decided, and texted this exciting development to her friends. Hub gave his tail a couple of sagacious wags, and that was it—dude was part of the family.

My relationship with Hub was always good. He was the Souls' dog and he loved us all equally, but I was the one who took him for long walks (and not just for a quick poop next to the mailboxes), and sometimes to the Beaches in Toronto, even to Skateboard tourneys. We understood each other. And sure, it would have been bitchin' to dress him in a Toes on the Nose T-shirt and get him on a shortboard, but that wasn't going to happen. Dude was—and still is—too cool for school.

The dynamic changed radically when I returned home after my accident. There'd be no more long walks or strolling along the boardwalk in the sunshine, but I had gained a superbrain and could communicate with Hub on a new and far out level.

The first thing he said to me was, *So . . . you got a king-sized chip on your shoulder? You going to be an unconscionable prick?*

Dude, I said. *This deal is temporary. I guaran-fucking-tee it.*

I hope you're right.

I am. So chill.

Dude, he said. *I define chill.*

Okay. Talking to dogs. Kind of gnarly. But you should know that it's not like a normal conversation. We're not talking in English, or in any spoken language. It's more like a sequence of symbols and feelings, like mental sign language, with a dash of intuition. This latter is something that all dog owners are familiar with. Ever look at your dog and sense—with eerie certainty—what they are thinking? There's a connection. Canines operate on a different bandwidth, and every so often are able to break through a human's cerebral firewall.

It's the same with all animals. You just have to recognize the bandwidth, which is one heck of a lot easier, I'll admit, without the firewall. But again, it comes down to the feather in front of the electric fan. It comes down to letting go.

So Hub struts into my groovy room a few days ago, slouches next to the Mork chair, his head propped on his front paws.

I'm in the doghouse, he said. *Again.*

What did you do? I asked.

Took a shit in the garden, he replied, and smiled. *Well, on the deck, actually. A sloppy one. Dad . . . not happy. He's out there with the hose right now.*

Nasty, I said.

Yeah, and the hose isn't so much washing it away as distributing it over a wider surface. I don't know what he's thinking. Still, that'll teach him for not taking me for a walk. It's been three days now.

Jesus, I said. *So that was a protest-shit?*

Hell yeah. A revolutionary shit. I'm like the Che Guevara of the dog world.

Un chien *Guevara,* I said.

Hub cracked another smile. *Che Grrrrrvara.*

We both sighed happily. Hub rolled on his side, tongue lolling. My head flopped to the right, tongue lolling. Best friends, man. No doubt.

You know if I was able to, I said, *I'd take you down to the Beaches, go check out the honeys.*

I know that, brother, Hub said. *Miss those days.*

Me too.

You told me it was a temporary deal. Hub's tail thumped once. Not a happy wag, but an agitated one. *That was eighteen months ago, dude. What gives?*

It's not like I haven't been trying, I said. It's painful how hard I've tried, and for how long, covering miles of cortical highway, around gyri, over sulci, looking for my exit. And sometimes I feel I'm getting close. Maybe I'll see a lighted off-ramp and I'll take it at thrilling speed, only to find that the road loops around to where I was before. It's like a frickin' Escher painting, man. You think you're going up, but you're only going down.

I'll miss our chats, though, Hub said. *You know, when you go back to being normal.*

I know, I said. *I'll have to give up all my superhero powers. It'll be like* Superman II, *when Kal-El has to become human so that he can be with Lois Lane.*

Whatever, man. I haven't seen Superman II.

Right. I shrugged. *Have you seen Schnoodleman II?*

That's not even funny, asswipe.

It's kinda funny.

You'd think, having the world's most incredible mind, that you'd be able to come up with a funny joke once in a while.

Any time I say the word schnoodle, it's funny.

Whatever.

No . . . really.

Hub lifted his foreleg and curled his lip. *Tell it to the paw.*

That got me laughing hard. Inside, of course. On the outside I stared at a faint water stain on the wall and drooled. Hub laughed, too, whuffling through his lips, his tail slapping the floor. We'd no sooner stopped than we heard Dad storm into the kitchen, cussing Hub and the Alaska-sized puddle of dogshit that was spreading across the rear deck. This got us laughing again, and so passionately that I could feel a tiny muscle in my jaw twitching.

There followed a moment's reverie, during which Hub yawned and licked his lips, and I composed a string quartet arrangement in the key of E minor.

I came in to see you last night, Hub said, cutting through the rapturous applause in my mind. *The lights were on but there was nobody home. Scratch that . . . the lights* weren't *on. You were gone, brother.*

Tell me about it, I said. *The atmosphere in the house was shitty. Has been for days. I jacked out of here. Went to Springsteen's pad. He had guests over. Elvis Costello. Tom Morello. They were jamming until four in the morning.*

Sweet, Hub said.

Then I sat on the edge of the Hudson and watched the sun rise over Manhattan's skyline.

Pretty, Hub said. *But I think something is going on, man. The vibe is heavy, and Mom was crying. All night.*

She gets upset, is all, I said, but my heart tripped in my chest and sent a flare of pain down my left side. *She cries a lot.*

Last night was different, though, Hub insisted. He sat up, looked at me, ears cocked. *Dad was quiet, too. Real sullen. Can't you jump into their minds to find out what's going on? A little psychic investigation?*

Come on, man, you know I don't like to do that. An involuntary, almost musical groan escaped me. My head rolled to the other side. Eyes fixed on the window now. A square of grey sky. *I see things I have no right seeing. It's totally uncool.*

Hub settled back down on his paws. *I'd just like to know that it's nothing serious. That's all.*

And even if I did break into their thoughts, I said. *What good would it do? I can't influence their decisions.*

This is true. There are, unfortunately, limits to my abilities. Just because I have access to other people's minds doesn't mean I can control their actions. Wish to hell I could. And sometimes I wish I could make their heads explode, like in *Scanners*. That would be awesome. But the reality is that humans operate within the tiny bubble of their conscious mind. Freud likened the psyche to an iceberg, with only 10% (the conscious) visible, and everything else (the ego, the superego, and the id—all the bitchin' stuff, in other words) hidden below the surface. It's a good metaphor, and for the most part accurate. But I prefer to think of the conscious mind as a wall. Solid and resilient. Not like a garden wall, that you can hop over whenever you wish. More like a barricade, heavily guarded, designed to protect, to keep unwanted things from entering, but also to prevent the essentials from leaving. The conscious mind is more like the Korean DMZ than the topmost portion of an iceberg, believe me.

I call it the Wall of the Self. It defines *you*. Built of genetics and experience, with each brick bonded by emotion. The things that make you strong. Every sane human being has this wall (it's what keeps you sane). I can jump into your mind and see it. I can rap my knuckles against it, too. But the only way to the other side—to get *inside* you, where I can govern your decisions and communicate at a telepathic level—is for you to invite me in. And that's not going to happen. Not if you're sane.

My wall was destroyed in the accident. Nothing left. To use Freud's metaphor, the iceberg has flipped for me. I now exist in the 90% you cannot see, with no access to the 10%. Thus, I can't walk or talk, but can dive into the warm waters of the pleasure principle at will, and totally rock the secondary process. I have access to my psychic energy and all my memories. My soul has grown wings and my brain—despite what Dr. Thinker says—runs at petaflop speeds.

There are instances when the wall is weakened. During sleep, when the subconscious comes bubbling to the surface, and in moments of impassioned creativity. Artists often talk about being in the zone—channelling their muse. The exterior world fades and they exist, for a delightful moment in time, in a different place. Essentially, they have called the guards down from the wall and opened a tiny window, but one that allows information to pass through. Creativity is all about opening the blockades. Jesus, it's the reason you're reading this now. There's a writer somewhere who thinks he's making this up, when all the time, I'm passing information through his creative window.

The inventive and the insane . . . the only people who let their walls down. Make of that what you will.

Animals have walls, too, but they're low and unguarded, which makes the exchange of information easier. Oftentimes their heads are empty, but some animals—dogs in particular—are sharp. Hub is no exception.

You said it yourself, man, he said, getting up and padding around to the other side of the bed so I could see him. *The atmosphere in the house has been shitty, and I for one don't dig it.*

I don't dig it, either, I said. *But it happens from time to time. Mom and Dad probably had an argument and it's still a little frosty. It'll pass. Trust me.*

You better be right.

Of course I'm right.

Spots of rain against the window, tapping, like some small creature trying to get out of a box. The sky a darker shade of grey. My soul ached to stretch its wings. I imagined a fawn ribbon of sand, The Beach Boys singing "Good Vibrations," and the refreshing tang of mojitos. I could have released there and then—*wanted* to—but I stayed with Hub. My buddy.

It's been a crazy week, he said. *What with the atmosphere, Fat Annie quitting, and nobody taking me for—*

What? I said. *Fat Annie quit? Are you serious?*

Dude, you didn't know?

Hell, no.

What, exactly, do you use that superbrain for?

I've been . . . I trailed off, feeling tears sting my eyes, even though they remained dry, didn't so much as blink. Fat Annie was my caregiver, and had been for eighteen months. She was stern (given to occasional acts of sweetness) yet undeniably effective, like Mr. Miyagi. I had the deepest respect for her. And yeah . . . love, too. Given the nature of our relationship, it was impossible not to form a bond. She came in most days for three hours—checked my vitals, maintained my PEG tube, took care of my toileting (by which I mean she changed my diapers and wiped my ass). She would sponge bathe me with a tenderness that sent shivers of goodness rolling through my body, massage my limbs to promote circulation, and do (painful, but necessary) assisted range of motion exercises to keep my joints flexible. She'd also administer my tinzaparin shot—a blood thinner that prevents deep vein thrombosis and pulmonary embolus. Ten thousand units injected into my abdomen (I have a neat little hard spot where the needle keeps going in—yeah, it's fun being me). If the weather was nice she would transfer me to my wheelchair and take me around the block, sometimes to the library, where it was quiet and the smell of books inspired daydreams. If it was too cold out, she'd sit me in my chair and read to me. After changing the sheets, she'd lift me back into bed, placing small pillows beneath my elbows and heels to prevent decubitus ulcers. And all the time—through all this care—she would talk to me. Normally. No baby-talk (you'd be surprised how many of my visitors revert to baby-talk: *Hey, Wessy . . . you feewing all wight? Awww, he's got an ickle bit of dwool on his chinny-winn*). No dumbing down or awkwardness. She spoke to me the way people should: like I'm a human being.

Yeah, I loved Fat Annie.

Her name wasn't even Annie. It was Georgina. Hub and I called her Fat Annie because she looked and dressed like Kathy Bates in *Misery*. We kept expecting her to call one of us a dirty bird, or walk in carrying a sledgehammer. Just our little joke. No malice intended. Fat Annie was the best. And now she's gone.

What the hell is going on? I said. *Why'd she quit?*

Hub frowned. *I love that the superbrain is asking the dog the questions.*

This is not good, Hub. What's my new caregiver going to be like?

I watched the rain hit the window.

I tell you, man, Hub said. *There's an uncool vibe in the air, and I don't like it.*

No, I said. *Me, either.*

Dad came in then, his face crossed with anger, his eyes little beads. Hub leapt to his feet and dashed from the room, his paws skating on the hardwood for a moment, like Scooby-Doo running from a ghost. Dad growled and aimed his foot at Hub's ass but missed.

¡Viva la revolución! Hub shouted over his shoulder, then was gone.

Dad paused for a moment, just looking at me, and I saw

his eyes mist over. He blinked and a solitary tear toppled down his cheek and disappeared into the fuzz of his beard. Then he pulled back my bedsheets and dressed me in my pyjamas, saying nothing, not as gentle with his hands as Fat Annie. He transferred me to my chair and wheeled me into the living room. No TV or radio on. Only the sound of the rain.

Dad sat on the sofa and we watched it come down together. Swags of deep grey, like stained lace, rippled past the window. Kiss of lightning.

"We love you, Wes," Dad said. "You know that, right?"

I imagined the rain reflected in my unblinking eyes.

"We love you so much."

Then Dad sort of flopped out of the sofa, dropped to his knees, and rested his head in my lap. He curled his arms around my waist and wept silently, as if he didn't want me to know that he was crying. But I could feel his shoulders rocking, his hands trembling, the uncomfortable warmth of his tears.

6. ON LOVE.

Can be confusing. Often overwhelming. Rock stars don't help; The Beatles sing, "All You Need Is Love," while Pat Benatar insists, "Love Is a Battlefield." And what the heck is with The Four Aces gushing, "Love Is a Many-Splendored Thing" in one ear, while Def Leppard are belting, "Love Bites" in the other? Doesn't make sense, right? Are we so obtuse when it comes to the sensibilities of the heart? Is love so complex an entity that nobody can fully grasp it? But we are the modern *Homo sapiens*. The theory of relativity. Man on the moon. PlayStation 3. The emperor penguin has a brain the size of a peach pit, yet their species know how to keep the love light burning. Don't believe me? Just watch *March of the Penguins*. Or *Happy Feet*. Why is it that Chilly Willy can ride the love train, when even the most intelligent among us are like fifth graders when it comes to hopping on board?

Lou Gramm—lead singer of the rock band Foreigner— once sang, "I Want to Know What Love Is." Well, I hope Mr. Gramm is reading this, because I'm going to tell him:

Love is simple. It is not a battlefield, and it doesn't

bite. It is not cruel or blind. It is simply an emotion. The complexities and imperfections are not love's; they are our own. Strip away the frustrations of living. Cast aside contempt and remorse. Make joy and anger walk the plank. Ditto optimism and trust. When you are left with nothing but love, you will see something breathtaking.

Now, I'm not telling you anything new here, and no doubt Mr. Gramm will be less than satisfied with my response. But bear with me, brotherman . . . this superbrain shiznit is useful for more than just astral projecting to Leafs games or watching Angelina Jolie take a shower.

The challenge isn't in understanding love, but in—to borrow from William Blake—cleansing the doors of perception . . . to see love how it truly is: a miniature sun. It provides heat and light, and the energy we need to survive. It may help, Mr. Gramm, to know that, like the sun, love needs a constant supply of fuel. I'm talking about fusion reaction, baby . . . the thermal collision of protons—*BAM!*—that sustain this brilliant source of energy. In other words . . . you stop throwing coal on the fire, and it's going to go out.

Corinthians 13 says that love never fails. This isn't true. Even our own sun will burn itself out one day (there are 5,766,923,227 years before you have to worry about that, though, so go ahead and buy that flat screen TV you were looking at). Love *can* fail, regardless of how much fuel there is to burn. We can't stop the wind from blowing, or the rain from falling. Sometimes the fire just dies. And fate . . . well, that's another subject.

But love is a miniature sun.

You want to feel that heat right now? Find a loved one

and throw your arms around them. They'll do the same to you, and—*BAM!*—protons collide, baby. It really is that simple. A science so elementary that penguins can understand it.

I know this not because I found love, but because I lost it.

Let me tell you what happened with Nadia.

7. OUR SONG.

My Bond girl, remember? *I want to be your Soul,* she had said.

She came to see me twice when I was in a coma. The first time she sat in the chair next to my bed, her hand clutching my fingers, occasionally stroking my hair. Her touch had always sent unreal sensations through my body, like threads of light in a plasma globe. Easy to imagine the fine hairs on her arms stiffening. But on this occasion, I had no light to give. I lay numb and unresponsive. A marionette with tubes for strings, waiting for someone to make me dance. Nadia leaned close enough to kiss me, whispered in my ear.

"Wake up, baby. Wake up for me."

She thought she could do it—that her voice, her touch, was like fairy dust, and would wake that deeply sleeping part of me. That it didn't happen changed something inside her. Very subtle, but enough for her to question our harmony. Enough to set a cool wind blowing across her miniature sun.

"I'm here." Her fingers tying bows in my hair. Unravelling them. Tying bows. "Wake up. Come back to me."

Tears had no effect on her beauty. In fact they enhanced it, the way imperfection can make a portrait more real. She would stop crying, eventually, but at that moment she was hurting. A nineteen-year-old raincloud. She curled her hand around my wrist and felt the vague tick of my pulse. It was all I could give her.

She visited again five days later—the day before she left for Toronto. Her hair was tied back, her face exposed. The lines of her cheeks seemed sharper, and her eyes too big. A sallow bead of light played on her brow. She kissed the bridge of my nose, delicately, before sitting down. Her hand looped into mine and for a long moment she sat silently, gazing at my sleeping face, listening to the chirp of the cardiac monitor.

"We were supposed to be at the beginning," she said. Her lips tightened. She looked away from me. The light through the window struck her glistening eyes. Not pink sunshine, but the pale silver of a Vancouver afternoon. "I had it all planned, baby. We were going to get married somewhere uncomfortably hot, then honeymoon until our bodies were shattered. You were going to open a surf shop while I deejayed. We'd have two children: Marvel and Calypso. A dog called Jesus. And we'd live happily ever after in a place where you could hear the palm fronds whisper, and where our garden was made of sand."

No tears. Maybe she was all cried out, or had found a ridge of inner strength, shaped like a saddle horn, that she clung to as the life she knew bucked and reared. With her hair drawn back she appeared austere. Harsh, almost. The effect of cooling winds. Still beautiful, but different from the girl who had sat in that seat five days before, her pieces held together by the weak glue of disbelief.

"Come back to me, baby," she said.

My IV line dripped saline.

Nadia let go of my hand. She reached into the beach bag she had brought in with her, took out her iPod and the Allen & Heath headphones she had been wearing when I first saw her. She leaned close and looped them over my ears, making sure they were comfortably placed. Then she plugged them into the iPod and found our song.

You may think—with us being so young, sexy, and kick-ass—that our song was something contemporary, blazing hot. Armin van Buuren, perhaps, or deadmau5. Maybe even one of the classics. "These Eyes," by The Guess Who, or just about anything by Bob Marley. Yeah, you may think that, but you'd be wrong. Nadia was a deejay, and her appreciation of music ran deep. Thus, our song was a l'il something from the nineties.

The *seventeen* nineties.

Beethoven's *Sonata pathétique*. The adagio movement. Special to us because that was when our protons first collided. Another memory I relive often, regardless of hurt. Every sweet sound. The smell of floor polish and lavender. My heart suddenly feeling as if it were filled with helium, climbing in my chest, wanting to carry me away. It was our third date. We'd done the SuperPoke thing on Facebook, I'd taken her to the movies and out for dinner. We'd kissed a few times, nothing more. But for Date #3 she'd invited me to her house (her parents were away for the weekend) and I knew that our relationship was about to hit the next level. I'd expected deep respect and intimacy—thinking, sensibly, that we were still a few dates away from falling in love.

I was wrong.

BAM!

Her parents own a kingly, neo-Georgian home in Rosedale (Daddy was—still is—one of the big wheels at CBC). Nadia kissed me at the door, made me feel welcome, but I still felt—coming from our modest home in small town Hallow Falls—out of place. Not uncomfortable with the splendour . . . just unfamiliar with it. I'd never been in a house that had a statue in the hallway before. A frickin' *statue.*

"This is the shit," I said to Nadia, and imagined the house shuddering with disdain. "I better not touch anything."

"Only me," Nadia said with a smile.

I kicked off my sneakers, dropped my backpack, and followed Nadia on the obligatory tour, which concluded not in her bedroom, as I had hoped (why delay the inevitable?), but in a room resplendent with funky artwork, sprigs of lavender, and a grand piano. An 1896 Steinway Model B, to be precise.

"The music room," she said brightly.

How could I resist? I stepped to the piano and tinkled a few of the high keys, matched the notes with a warbling false. Nadia looked at me, one eyebrow raised.

"What do you get when you drop a piano down a mine shaft?" I asked.

She shrugged.

"A-flat minor." *Tinkle-tinkle!*

"Funny," she said. "You get that joke from a Christmas cracker?"

"The great Fozzie Bear," I said. "Wocka Wocka."

Half a smile. "You're playing B-flat, though. Now C . . . now B-flat again."

I stopped tinkling. "You play?"

"A little."

"Show me what you got."

She considered for a moment, biting her lower lip, looking from my expectant face to the piano's immaculate keyboard, then back to me. I thought a little shyness was creeping in, but this wasn't the case; she was actually afraid I would think her uncool. All I had really seen of Nadia was a hottie who could kick the decks and kiss like a soul-breaker, but now I was going to see the flip side. The rich man's daughter, who sat with her knees together and her chin high. Montessori schooling and tennis trophies. Piano lessons from the age of four . . . continuing until she was old enough to rebel, get a tramp stamp, and play music of a different kind.

"I don't know what to play," she said, hesitating.

"Doesn't matter," I said. "Play anything."

She sighed and looked at me, her eyes deep and warm. *This is who I am,* that look said. *Take it or leave it.* I replied by touching her cheek, curling a wisp of hair behind her ear, making her smile. She sat at the piano, her back straight, her small feet poised above the pedals.

"Okay," she said.

I didn't know what to expect. As I've said, the Nadia I knew was punkier . . . wilder. This was a different version, but—as I was about to discover—no less alluring. She placed her fingers on the keys and they suddenly looked more elegant. Those fingers had tousled my hair and set turntables on fire, but now they were as light as motes of dust. This wasn't the only change. A calm had fallen across her face. Her whole demeanour settled. She went from a river, tumultuous and white, to a lake, serene and blue.

And then she started to play.

Within moments, everything inside me lifted, teased into flight by notes as delicate as the fingers that played them. My skin flushed with sensation. My mouth dropped open. Heart floating in my chest as I breathed shallow sips of air. I'd never known anything so beautiful. Not just the melody, but to see Nadia so transformed, and to feel her oneness with the music . . . it was astounding. And as those notes tiptoed in the air, coalescing with the lavender to kiss my senses, I *felt* it—beauty and euphony activating gravitational collapse, the build-up of heat, a chain reaction. It was happening, beyond my control. Nuclear fusion. My sun forming.

Nadia played the final note and it faded from the air, leaving something behind. An intangible. A kind of . . . sweetened silence. She stood up and stepped toward me. Punky again, but different. Chewing her lower lip. Dark eyes shimmering. I took her hands, touched her fingers, as if they couldn't be real.

"Beethoven," she said.

I nodded hopelessly.

"*Sonata pathétique*," she added. "Second movement. Adagio cantabile."

"Yeah," I said, as if I knew that. I stroked her fingers, expecting them to fade perfectly, like the music.

"It's pretty," Nadia said.

"Breathtaking," I said.

Another sweet silence while we stood beside the grand piano, hands clasped, looking at each other. The heat was suffocating. We kissed, eventually, and then consummated the moment. Not the fumbling, over-excited coitus of youth, but a considerate union. Two mirrors facing one another, reflecting to the point where light ran out.

Thirteen months later, with a cardiac monitor ticking away my broken life—a clock with no hands—Nadia placed her headphones over my ears and played *Sonata pathétique*'s second movement . . . her final, desperate attempt to reach me, and to rescue a future with Marvel and Calypso—our garden made of sand.

"Come back," she said again.

I gunned the Soulmobile through the rain-slick streets of my coma. Lightning in the sky and Dr. Quietus in my rearview mirror. I screeched onto the Ego Ideal, where blank towers loomed above me and the traffic signals were caught between stop and go. Dr. Quietus put his foot to the floor and closed the distance between us. His voracious engine howled.

I've got you this time, Westlake Soul, he said, and cackled.

I tried to go faster . . . to get everything I could out of my failing machine. I took a hard left turn onto Preconscious Boulevard and Dr. Quietus was right behind me. His headlights filled the Soulmobile with dreadful light.

There's no getting away.

In the rearview mirror, I watched missile launchers unfold from his fenders, hood, and roof—each one loaded with a 15-Megaton WS Heart Stopper. He cackled again. More lightning in the sky, illuminating empty sidewalks, the falling rain. I crushed the accelerator, knowing there was no way out . . . and suddenly the Auditory Cortex light was flashing in the HUD. I hit the button and several thousand decibels of *Sonata pathétique* shook my comatose world.

Nadia, I thought.

The music gave the Soulmobile a boost. Rainwater fanned from the rear tires and Dr. Quietus's headlights shrank to pinpricks. My heart cannoned as the windows of dead skyscrapers blew out. Deep cracks raced through their structures, weakening them. I saw one building—I think it was the Arbor Vitae Exchange—sag like a tired muscle, and then partially collapse as I raced by. I looked for Nadia. Her face on a billboard. Her name on a street sign. Nothing. Only the music, inciting emotion. Notes leading me like small men running on a track. I took an exit to the Pleasure Principle and caned it at unspeakable miles per hour.

Where are you?

I imagined delicate fingers touching piano keys. Those same fingers touching me.

NADIA!

No sign of her. I smeared tears from my eyes, and then Dr. Quietus was behind me again. His machine purred, smooth and efficient. Missiles locked on. He fired— cackling wildly—and arrows of light bloomed in the rearview mirror, shooting toward me, trailing smoke.

This is the end of the road, Westlake Soul!

Three seconds to impact. The supervillain boomed laughter.

The music—our song—embraced me, as it always had. I recalled how my sun had formed, and burned still.

Two seconds . . .

The sun, I thought. *Up.*

Through the black rags thrown over the city, I saw a crescent of red light.

One second to impact.

Up, I thought again, and punched a button on the console labelled, *PSYCHEJECTOR*. The Soulmobile's roof snapped open and my seat thrust upward. I soared into the night, surrounded by music. Below me, Dr. Quietus's missiles hit the Soulmobile and it exploded in a ball of white flame— *KA-BLAAM!*—spraying stellate cells and afferent neurons.

Lightning jagged and the music started to fade.

NADIA! I screamed with everything I had, my lungs full of glass.

Dr. Quietus's black machine rumbled into the distance. I heard him cry out in rage—vowing to return—as I arced over the Pleasure Principle. I searched the sky, looking for that glimpse of the sun, but saw only cloud.

NADIA!

No sign of her. No way out of this dark city. I turned my face to the sky. Rain fell into my eyes as the music faded.

In my hospital room, Nadia clicked the stop button on her iPod and took the headphones from my ears. She sat a moment longer, looking at me, dreams slipping from her heart like snow off a roof. Still no tears. Only those big eyes and sharp lines. More the girl at the piano than the cool chick beatmatching tracks.

"I don't know what—" she started, but stopped. Pressed a knuckle to her lips. She never finished that sentence. If only she knew how desperately I was trying to reach her.

Those two words again: *if only*.

She put her iPod and headphones back into her beach bag and stood up. The soles of her sneakers squeaked on the floor as she walked toward the door. One final look over her shoulder, the last wedge of snow sliding from her roof. I lay among my tubes and lines like a torn parachute. My cardiac monitor chirped. The door closed softly behind her.

So Nadia returned to her home in Rosedale with a trail of broken pieces, and I remained in my empty city—until I discovered a thread of light between two buildings, once robust, that had crumbled and collapsed against one another. I powered through the narrow gap. Opened my eyes.

I was transferred, almost immediately, to Toronto Western Hospital, which meant that I got more visitors. Niki came two or three times a week. She showed me pictures of Hub and her various new boyfriends, and bitched to me about the shittiness of life, and how Mom and Dad had her doing twice as many chores for the same allowance. Her visits were always such a highlight. Nonetheless, I longed to reach out, pull her into my arms, and kiss her bratty little face. Darryl would drop by. Usually once a week. He never had much to say, though. Inane comments that I might once have found interesting: *Got some dope new ink, bitch. Right shoulder. Tribal fire with boards bustin' out of it. Fuckin' dope, bitch*. Mostly he would just stare at me, as if I were a new breed of creature. Something no man had ever seen before. On one occasion, he showed me some porn on his iPhone. On another—clearly bored—he ate a flower.

Nadia came, too.

One last time.

I would have preferred that she didn't come at all, with her new short haircut and the cold rock that used to be her sun. The last time she saw me—that glance over the shoulder in my Vancouver hospital room—I was (sort of) sleeping. Granted, my face was bruised and scraped, and

I was plugged in to various life-monitoring/sustaining apparatus, but I was still sleeping, thus relatively normal. Awake, though, with my head cricked sideways and frothy sputum on my chin, I was shocking. Not only that, but a nurse had cut my lovely blond hair to keep it from falling into my eyes. A brutal cut, too—sheared me to the scalp in places. Frickin' Vidal Sassoon, she was not.

It was the worst possible time for Nadia to visit. I was ashamed. Horrified.

Don't look at me, I implored her.

"Westlake," she said. Two steps toward my bed, then she stopped, covered her eyes with one hand. Her lower lip pooched out. She broke, tears sparkling through the cracks of her fingers, shoulders trembling. Her hand had slipped from that saddle horn of strength. I ached to fly away. I ached to hold her.

The vein in my temple throbbed. All the emotion I could offer.

I don't want you to see me like this, I said. *Go away, baby. Please, just go—*

My sun flared painfully.

"Sorry," Nadia said, wiping her eyes, stroking mascara across her cheekbones. She was sorry for crying. For not being strong. I wanted her to be sorry for coming. She looked at the plain white ceiling, as if she'd find composure there. Impulsively, I leapt into her mind. It sounded like a subway train—like the wave that had killed me. Her thoughts were not images. More like shaped feelings. I deciphered them and saw our former togetherness . . . pink sunshine . . . how I looked in her eyes: a pale, partial thing.

Just leave. Please. I threw these thoughts at her. Vehemently. They thudded off her wall like stones. *I don't WANT you here. I can't take it.*

She took a seat, not beside my bed, but in the corner, where I couldn't see her. This wasn't ideal, but it was better. I could still hear her, of course. Shaky breaths, uncomfortable movements. Long minutes passed. I prayed—of all my superhero powers—to be invisible, and wondered if I could mentally refract enough light to at least fade into the white hospital sheets. I tried, of course, but nothing happened. I was too emotional to concentrate and had to settle for the room dimming when a cloud moved over the sun.

Literally. Figuratively.

"I can't do this," Nadia said. I couldn't see her, but knew she was crying again. "It's just too much. I can't bear to see you like this, and I'm not strong enough to handle it."

You are, I said bitterly. *You just don't want to.*

"Can you even hear me, Westlake?"

Of course I can hear you.

"Do you even understand?"

More than you realize.

And I did, but not because of my super intelligence. I didn't need to pluck thoughts from her mind to know that the love was gone. She emitted no heat, no energy. This hurt so deeply that I felt it in my spine. A bleak fluid. Coupled with the shame, I could have died—thrown myself at Dr. Quietus's feet. And yet my sun still flared, trying to provide light for us both.

Could I blame her, though? I have pondered this so often since, and asked myself what I would do in her situation.

Nadia was young and beautiful. She had everything to look forward to, and I could offer nothing. Furthermore, I didn't know what *I* wanted (other than my body, of course—my *life*). I loved her too much to lose her . . . too much for her to stay.

If only she had been stronger. It would have made it easier for us both. *If only* she had held my hand, and told me that we would still have our garden made of sand. I needed her faith, but it was as cold as the rock that had once been her sun. She didn't want to be my Soul anymore. My pale, partial image had eclipsed everything. I was already dead to her.

Just get out of here. I wished she could see how angry I was. How desperately hurt. *Please, Nadia . . . you're not helping.*

"I didn't know if I should come," she said, her voice a little firmer. "But I need to end this. I need to move on."

I groaned involuntarily and my head rolled to the other side so that—dammit—I could see her again. Sitting on the edge of the chair. Knees together. Purse in her lap because she didn't plan on staying long. Her short, painfully cute haircut much cooler than mine.

Still breathtaking. That was the adjective I had used when she played Beethoven's *Sonata pathétique*, referring not to her playing (which *was* dope), but to *her*. And despite her lack of faith, and her wanting to *end this,* it still applied.

My eyes tracked toward the sunlight like two lazy flowers and a long thread of spit hung from my lower lip. Inside, I was coming apart. Thrashing and weeping. I wanted to release—fly to the ocean and let every wave crash against my bruised soul. But I stayed with Nadia, because some things have to be endured. As much as it hurt, I needed to end this, too.

This is who I am, I thought, remembering the pristine girl at the piano. *Take it or leave it.*

She stood up, wiped her eyes again, then glided toward my bed. I could smell her body. The familiarity was overwhelming. Her hand inched forward, tentative, then curled around my forearm. I expected the cardiac monitor to explode, but it didn't sound any different.

"I would have married you," she said. "A thousand times over. I *wanted* to. You know that, right?"

I know that, I said.

"And I don't regret one single moment I spent with you."

The hurt . . . I just wanted it to end. And still I threw my heat at her—even tried to twitch the muscle in my forearm, desperately wanting her to feel *something*.

"If I could change just one thing," she said, more tears spilling onto her cheekbones. "I would go back to that pink morning in Tofino. I would pin you to the bed and stop you from leaving. And you'd be . . ." She let go of my forearm, used both hands to wipe her face. Her body jerked as she broke again. "You'd . . ."

She couldn't finish.

I know. I wanted to hold her. One last time. To feel her body in my arms. To give her my strength. *I know, baby.*

"It wasn't supposed to *be* like this," she spat, and for just one second that cold rock inside her glowed. A momentary light. Then it was gone. She shook her head, perhaps at the unfathomable cruelty of the world, and stepped toward the door.

I listened to the tears fall on my soul. A sound like the

high notes on a piano. B-flat, C, B-flat again. The world laughs at you sometimes. Wocka Wocka.

"Goodbye, Westlake." She looked over her shoulder one final time, just as she had in Vancouver. "I'll always remember you."

I couldn't speak. Not even inside. I watched her leave forever and then took flight. A breathless, heartbroken rush of light. To the ocean, where we roared together. I let the waves rush through me, knowing they couldn't hurt me any more than they already had. Then I soared toward the sun, breaking through the exosphere into outer space, until—ninety-three million miles from home—I arrived at my destination. I threw my arms open and let it burn me. Ten thousand Fahrenheit. The world's light. The world's *love*. But still it couldn't make up for what I had lost.

8. A Week in the Life.

The tension remained thick and uncomfortable in the Soul homestead. Hub was right; some unrighteous shit was going down, and there were too many silences for me to get to the bottom of it. Dad and Mom would often be in the same room, looking at each other, but rarely communicating. The occasional stiff smile, perhaps. Maybe a hug. One time Mom started crying on Dad's shoulder and he stroked her hair—as loving as I had seen him in quite some time— whispering, "It's okay, sweetheart . . . everything will be okay," over and over, until his throat was choked with emotion and he couldn't get the words out anymore. I held them both, wishing they could feel me.

Niki isn't the most astute seventeen-year-old in the world. I've often thought that, if she were a bird, she'd be the kind that would fly into a window. Pretty feathers, but a little bit dim. Even so, she picked up on the vibe, as well. One evening, at the dinner table, and during a particularly leaden silence, she slammed her knife and fork down so hard that her plate almost tipped over.

"Like," she started, "what the *fuck* is going on?" Then

she clapped a hand over her mouth and her eyes switched between Mom and Dad with a clicking sound, reminding me of those executive ball clickers you find in . . . well, executive ball clickers' offices.

I hovered over the mashed potatoes, eager to hear my parents' reply. Equally eager to see them haul Niki over the coals for dropping the F-bomb at the dinner table. Given the mood in the house, I thought it possible they'd be burying her in the garden at sundown.

Mom and Dad exchanged a look. I saw Dad's jaw flex as he gritted his teeth. Mom gave him a near-imperceptible shake of the head, then went back to her Polish sausage.

"Eat your dinner, Phereniki," Dad said. The use of her full name indicated his displeasure, but it was still a monumentally disappointing reaction. I thought food was going to fly. Maybe knives, too. Niki lowered her hand and went back to her meal, incredulous that she had gotten off so lightly. Her eyes continued to click from right to left, though, still wary of being sucker-slapped by a half-pound of grilled kielbasa.

But more disappointing than not seeing a reenactment of Passchendaele over the dinner table was the fact that my parents didn't answer Niki's question. Did this mean that it was too serious to discuss with her, or not serious enough? I waited through another uncomfortable silence, hoping someone would speak. But no one did. Only the clash of cutlery on dinner plates. Eventually, I gave up and reentered my body—went inside and surfed the universal wave function. When I emerged, the house was dark and sleeping.

So I consoled myself with the knowledge that, if I

needed to know, I would know. Wasn't much consolation, to be fair, but short of violating my parents' minds—their secrets—it was all I could do.

It'll pass, I had said to Hub. *Trust me.*

I believed this, but it was taking longer than usual. Even when Dad had fried the old home computer with viruses from porn sites, and Mom had thrown her favourite Laughing Buddha ornament at him, it hadn't taken this long for the icicles to thaw. Thank God I could release, and did so often—preferring ghost-like wanderings to the bum vibe at home.

Whatever was wrong, I didn't think it spelled the end for our tight family unit. Mom and Dad had weathered worse (me, for instance), so I had little doubt the mood would improve. Maybe Mom had found an inappropriate text on Dad's cell phone. Something to—or from—one of the secretaries in his office. Or maybe his performance at work had dipped and he'd been given his marching orders. I saw no point in trying to guess the problem. It could be one of many things, or an accumulation of petty annoyances. The deep ocean of married life. Sometimes smooth enough to skip stones on. Sometimes wild enough to ride. My concern was that it was because of me—that, when you stripped everything away, I would be bedded there like a leech. Hell, I know the situation; they love me, but I am hard work. *Emotionally draining.* That could be my epitaph: *Here lies Westlake Soul. Son, brother, surfer. A badass dude, but EMOTIONALLY DRAINING.* Had Dad sought comfort in the arms of a secretary, or failed to secure lucrative contracts, because his home life was a tower of stress? Had Mom been getting a little too familiar with the Crown

Royal because wiping the sleepy sand from my eyes every morning was all too much?

I went to where the world was light, and where there was hope. A field full of poppies in Belgium. A pearl-white waterfall in the heart of the Amazon rainforest. Rescue centres and moments of triumph. Maternity wards and kindergartens, where children—babies, really—held hands and absorbed the planet through wide, beautiful eyes. I rode elephants across the Serengeti, and swam with a pod of orcas in the deep of the Atlantic. I knew I was turning my back on the problems at home, but the escape was like a balm.

Darryl came to see me, which was unexpected (he has only visited me at home a couple of times—he finds it difficult, seeing me the way I am), but welcome. His empty-headed manner helped soothe the tension, albeit temporarily. Mom and Dad—never big Darryl fans— threw their arms around him before he had even kicked off his sneakers.

"Whoa," he said, grinning sweetly. "Good to see you, too."

He dropped by so he could show off his new car. A 2011 Chevy Camaro, straight out of the showroom. Dad lifted me into my chair and we went out to see it as a family. Even Niki came out, somehow lured from watching The Situation flex his abs on *Jersey Shore*. It was, all told, a nice moment. Darryl's new car was mean and green, easy on the eye, but I found the smiles and laughter—after such a long period of sullenness—more appealing.

After much complimentary cooing over such things as the Synergy Green paint job and the twenty-inch rims

(Hub wanted to piss on those rims as a left-libertarianism revolt against the exploitative ideology of a capitalist society—I told him not to spoil the good vibe), Darryl offered everybody a ride. But he looked at me awkwardly, realizing that I would have to sit up front, flopping around and drooling all over the interior. Mom registered Darryl's expression and came to his rescue.

"You guys go," she said, clasping the push handles of my chair. "I'll take Wes back inside. Maybe he can . . ." She trailed off, as if she had forgotten what she was going to say. A glance at Dad. An uncertain smile.

"Sure. Okay. Whatever," Darryl said. Carefree words, but he spoke and moved too quickly for them to have substance. He was behind the wheel, gunning the engine, before Mom had even turned my chair around. Niki hopped in the back and Dad in the passenger seat. They ripped out of the driveway in a flash of green.

Mom wheeled me back inside with Hub padding along behind, grumbling under his breath. She pushed me through to the living room, where I sat in a belt of sunlight while she read *The Globe and Mail*. I watched her for a moment. My beautiful mother, holding her figure at forty-eight, but with too many creases on her brow. Not enough laugh lines. I reached for her and, coincidentally, she looked up from her paper.

What is it, Mom? I asked, still reaching. *What's been getting you down?*

No reply, but she kept looking at me, studying me, the way I used to study the ocean—gauging break and current—before going in. I would ask just one question, almost without fail (and the one morning I didn't ask, it cost me everything): *What do I need to do?* Without reading her mind, or needing to, I could see that same question flickering in her eyes. As clear as moonlight on a lake.

I know it's breaking heavy, Mom, I said. *But you just have to stay focused. You have to ride this wave out.*

I tried to do something to convey my support. Soften my eyes. Open my hand. Twitch my lip in the merest of smiles. But the motor cortex was a ghost town, and though I ran through it screaming for help, I got no response. Not a shutter clapping in the breeze. Not even a tumbleweed skittering along the barren street. Hub came in and helped me out—jumped onto the sofa next to Mom and rested his head on her thigh. She put the newspaper down. Stroked his golden fur.

Thanks, I said to him.

He gave his tail a single happy thump. Mom managed half a smile and scratched behind his ear. And then she said, suddenly:

"What do you want, Westlake?"

The question surprised me, mainly because the answer was obvious, but also because she had asked with such earnestness, as if expecting me to swivel toward her, steeple my fingers, and provide a detailed, eloquent response. I did these things, of course, but *inside*, where she couldn't see them . . . where I was alive.

I want the cloudy vibe to go away, I said. Sunlight winked off my wheelchair's aluminum tubing. A single spark of life. *I want you and Dad to smile again. Niki, too. But most of all, I want to recover—re-flip the iceberg and go back to the way things used to be. And I* will *do it, Mom. It's so hard, and it's taking far too long . . . but I'll get there. I promise.*

I tried to push this bubble of optimism toward Mom, transfer it via the particles between us. An emotive shockwave. Hub felt it—slapped his tail again. Maybe Mom felt it, too, although her reaction was not what I had hoped for. Her face rippled. Her tears flowed. I couldn't bear it. In a whisper I was gone, tearing from my broken body, into the clear sky above our house. Higher still, a ribbon in the cold air, until Hallow Falls stretched below me—parks and parking lots, neat roads lined with maples, houses as colourful as children's building blocks. I spied a green Camaro turning onto Ernest Clayton Street, recalled the brief but welcome relief that Darryl's visit had brought, and swept toward it like rain. Within a heartbeat I was sitting in the backseat, next to Niki, hungry for an atmosphere that wasn't soaked in tears.

Darryl was showing off his upgraded sound system. Lady Gaga thrilled the speakers at light-bending volume. Niki was digging it, dancing as freely as she was able behind her seatbelt, while Dad nodded politely. He had never looked so old. I could see the small white hairs in his beard trembling.

Darryl finally turned the volume down and they drove a few blocks listening to the engine purr.

"She's sweet, eh?" Darryl asked, turning onto Main, heading toward home. I braced to fly away—didn't want to go home yet.

"Sick," Niki said.

"It's a nice car, Darryl," Dad said. "You be careful. And drive the speed limit. Police are always more likely to pull over a car that stands out like this, particularly if it's being driven by someone who wears his baseball cap sideways."

"I'm always careful," Darryl said. He flicked Dad a cautious glance. "Especially after what happened to Westlake. Shit like that makes you stop and think. You don't always get a second chance, right?"

"Right," Dad said. He pursed his lips.

Another two blocks where the only sound was the engine growling, and then Darryl—speaking as if the words had been shot from his larynx by a miniature cannon—said: "I thought he was going to get better if anyone could it would be Westlake no doubt eh?"

Dad frowned. "Take a breath, Darryl, and say that again."

Darryl nodded, took a breath. "I thought Westlake was going to get better," he said. "I was *sure* of it."

"Yes," Dad said, and sighed. "We thought so, too."

"I can't stand to see him like that."

"I know."

"But things will get easier?" Darryl raised the intonation of the last word, turning it into a question.

Dad looked out the window. I didn't think he would answer. Perhaps he hadn't registered the subtle shift in Darryl's tone—thought it was a statement rather than a question, and was content to let it hang. But then he said, almost too soft to hear:

"Not before they get a lot harder."

That vibe again. Instant. As if Darryl had steered his brand new Camaro into an oversized bag of gloom. I didn't hang around. Blink of an eye and I was gone, leaving my woeful family far behind. I flew until even my soul was breathless, finally coming to rest in some florid treetop where countless birds sang brightly.

So I escaped the atmosphere, for the most part. I missed my family, but I didn't miss their tears. I'd zip back every now and then—chat with Hub, see if things were better—and then leave again. And although partying in Ayia Napa and cliff diving in Acapulco was dope, I would have taken a pass—a thousand times over—to catch my parents smile.

They interviewed potential new caregivers while I was gone. Three of them. I know this because Hub told me, and because I overheard my parents talking about it, albeit briefly, on one of the few occasions I was home.

"I'm out Thursday night," Dad said. They were loading the dishwasher together. Plates and dishes rattled angrily. "Going to Dan's to listen to the White Album on vinyl. There may be alcohol. Giggle weed, too."

"You can't Thursday," Mom said. "We're interviewing, remember?"

"Oh," Dad said. His lower lip turned down, and then his upper lip flared as he tried to wedge a mug between two glasses. The muscles in his forearm tightened.

"You're going to break something," Mom said.

"What's the point, anyway?" Dad snapped. He tossed the mug into the other side of the rack, chipping the handle.

"The point?" Mom asked.

"In interviewing."

Mom looked at him squarely, her eyes wide and pale. "I haven't decided anything," she said.

"I think you have. We both have."

She shook her head, jaw clenched.

"Can't you interview without me?"

"No, I can't," Mom replied. "We make every decision—*every* one—together. That was the agreement."

Dad slammed in the final plate and walked away, and Mom stood there for a moment, trying not to cry.

I thought Dad's question—*what's the point?*—a peculiar one. He obviously felt that Fat Annie could not be replaced, but unless he and Mom wanted to assume caregiver duties (not a chance, baby), she would have to be. Dad knew this, of course. He was just pissed about having to miss a night with Dan and The Beatles.

Can't say I blame him; it's good to get away.

So yeah, tough times in the Soul homestead, with a particularly demanding week culminating in an argument of epic proportions. I didn't see it, but Hub said it was bad. Everybody crying. Things broken. And then, the very next day, a dash of much-needed good news. A suggestion of hope.

Hub came skating into my room so fast that he couldn't stop. He slid into the Mork chair with a thud that flipped him onto his back.

Son of a bitch!

Hub . . . dude, you okay?

He laughed, shook his head. *Wipeout, huh? Goddamn hardwood floors.*

So what is it? I asked. *Is the house on fire? Little Timmy stuck down the well?*

Don't be an asshole, he said, picking himself up and padding over to me with his tail flapping. *I came to tell you that your new caregiver starts tomorrow.*

Okay, I said. *And you needed to race in here like Usain Bolt for that?*

But you haven't seen her, Hub said, and his grin flashed like a billboard in Vegas. *Dude . . . she's the bomb.*

The bomb?

He nodded, long tongue flopping, and I smiled inside. It's always nice to see a pretty face, and I found myself hoping that my new caregiver's hands were as kind as Fat Annie's—that she would take me out sometimes. To the library. The park. Some alone-time with a pretty girl. Sweet as Tupelo honey. Just what I needed.

Not that I wasn't aware of the reality. . . .

Let's hope, I said to Hub, *that she has a weakness for ex-surfing champions in permanent vegetative states.*

Aww, shaddup, Hub said. *She's going to fall head over heels for you, man. How could she not?*

Which just goes to show that, when it comes to undying faith and love, you need look no further than the family dog.

9. YVETTE.

I still don't know why Fat Annie quit. Maybe she found a less stressful job. A librarian, perhaps. Fat Annie loved the library. Or maybe she won the lottery and moved to the Florida Keys. I could have found out, if I really wanted to—astral projected to her home in Mathias to see if they were loading up the U-Haul, or hopped into her car as she drove to work one morning. Easy enough, but what would knowing change? It might make me feel worse, if anything. Abandoned. Besides, I respected Fat Annie too much to invade her privacy. Done is done, baby. I know that better than anyone. All you can do is move on.

I was sure I'd miss her, though. I had a teacher in Grade Seven—Mrs. Moon—who was as strict as they come, and loved to heap on the homework. But she was *good*, and every now and then would give you a little smile that warmed your heart. I didn't think I'd miss her when she retired, but dammit I *did*, because, even at such a young age, I recognized that I'd lost something valuable. Mrs. Moon wasn't the hip teacher, or the funny one, but she had my best interest— my education—at heart, and you don't meet many people like that in the course of a lifetime. Not even teachers.

Fat Annie was similar to Mrs. Moon in many ways. Brusque but efficient, with moments of tenderness that could throw bluebirds into your day. And yeah, I *do* miss her . . . just not as much as I thought I would.

The reason is simple.

Yvette.

She's the bomb, Hub had said, and he was right.

Light brown hair that spills across one side of her face when it isn't tied back. Eyes that could have been chipped from some rare mineral, so full of flicker it's difficult to tell if they're green or blue. Her shoulders are narrow, but her arms perfectly toned. Skin so smooth it shines, and features that are often described as elfin: small mouth, high cheekbones, and those eyes—almond-shaped—of mysterious colour. She is perfect in every way. The kind of unflawed beauty that demands you stare.

Yeah . . . my new caregiver.

Needless to say, I didn't release the morning she was due to start. The vibe in the house was as taut as a drum skin, with each move or word creating a solemn percussive sound, but I stayed put. I didn't want to miss Yvette's arrival. Mom (in tears) brushed my hair, tucking loops behind my ears, the way she used to when I was five years old. A beautiful boy with dancing eyes, and his whole life ahead of him. I wondered if that same boy cartwheeled through Mom's mind as she ran the brush through my long hair, and then I heard a car turning into our driveway. I stretched from my body just enough to see a yellow VW Beetle pull up beside Mom's Acura, then snapped back as Hub came sliding into the room.

Dude, she's here, he said, wagging his tail, making circles. He was so excited that he actually barked. *She's here, Wes. She's really here*.

Yeah, I said. *I know*.

I'm so pumped.

I can see that.

Mom stopped brushing my hair, then plucked a Kleenex from a box on my nightstand and used it to dry her eyes. The doorbell rang. Hub expressed his excitement with uncharacteristic yapping. He bolted into the hallway and Mom followed, snapping at him to shut the hell up. I sat nervously, thankful that my hair was looking good and that I didn't have any goobers crusting the insides of my nostrils.

You may recall me saying that, with Nadia, it was not love at first sight. She was cool to the extreme, in her tiny jean skirt and Donna Karan shades, but the love didn't kick in—didn't *form*—until I heard her play piano. Yvette was different, though. *Cool* wasn't a word that immediately sprang to mind. She came dressed for work, after all. Comfortable slacks and a white blouse. Yet she had an inner light that made the bright yellow walls and blue ceiling seem lacklustre in comparison. It *boomed* from her, inspiring incredible feeling. Words like *tender*, and *warm*, and *kind*, spun layers around her. This was how she was formed. Like a pearl. A perfect pearl.

And yeah, that light fused with mine. Immediately. *BAM!* A chain reaction. I was lost to her. Would do anything for her.

"This is Westlake," Mom said, leading Yvette into my groovy room. She stood at the foot of my bed, professional and pretty, her hair drawn back from her face and tied with a red band. I ripped out of my body for one second to look at myself, positive that I would see some reaction: my eyes wide and excited, perhaps, or my legs trembling as something overwhelming zigzagged through me. But there was nothing. I simply lay there, as motionless as a stain, with my hair tucked behind my ears the way Mom had left it.

"Westlake," Mom said. "This is your new caregiver, Yvette."

Hi, Yvette, I said. How could I sound so cool?

"Hello, Westlake," Yvette said, smiling. She was looking into my eyes. Looking for *me*. She recognized, right away, that there was someone inside. Another reason to love her.

A brief, slightly awkward pause, and then Mom was showing Yvette where she would find everything she needed. Bedsheets and clothes in the closet (a modest wardrobe, consisting of shorts and T-shirts for the summer, track pants and sweaters for the winter), pads and pillows in this drawer, BP cuff, latex gloves, and first aid kit in the next drawer down, PEG tube paraphernalia over here. "We keep his formula in the kitchen," Mom explained. "I'll show you where in a moment." Laundry basket in the en suite, along with—obviously—all bathroom essentials. "We usually give Wes a dip in the bath and wash his hair once a week. You don't have to do that, but Georgina, our previous caregiver, would sponge bathe him whenever she came in." Towels on the rack. Diaper genie here. Fresh diapers and baby wipes over here. "Get out of the way, Hub—Jesus Christ." And then Mom took Yvette through to the kitchen, with Hub following close behind, flapping his tail.

I was left alone, staring at an empty space that, only moments before, Yvette had filled so sweetly. Traces of her fragrance remained. Coconut and apple. A hint of tea tree oil. The fresh scent of her laundry detergent. I'd been in her company for less than three minutes. She had spoken only two words to me. Yet my fabulous mind was already thinking of ways I could get her to fall in love with me. Not the kind of affection that nurses often develop with their patients . . . but *real* love. Like Lennon and Yoko. Joanie and Chachi. A tall order, even for me, and another reason—if one were needed—to battle my way to a full recovery.

My thoughts veered into a romantic fantasy (in my able-bodied days it would be called a masturbation fantasy) that barely gained steam before Yvette, Mom, and Hub returned to my room. I snapped back to reality and tried to smile. Maybe tip a wink. No movement, of course. Not even a twitch. But Yvette made everything good by smiling at me. Straight white teeth. Lips brushed with a clear gloss. Suddenly I forgot all about the cloud hanging over *casa* Soul.

"Okay, Westlake," Yvette said.

You can call me Wes, I said.

"You can call him Wes," Mom said.

"Okay, Wes." Yvette curled her fingers over the footboard of my bed. I looked for a ring and saw only a thin silver band on her right pinky. "How about we start by getting you out of those pyjamas?"

Hub chuckled and left the room. Mom smiled. After so many clouds, this was beautiful to see.

"Sound good?" Yvette asked.

Everything inside me grinned. *Grab your Crayolas and colour me tickled pink*, I said.

WESTLAKE SOUL

I stayed close to home during those first few days. I didn't want to be too far away from Yvette, and made sure I was locked into my body during her visits. She does everything with exquisite care, and her touch amazes me—both strong and tender. The way she will tilt my head to one side while she shaves me, her fingertips on my lips. And when she bathes me . . . long strokes with the sponge, over my chest, gently around the tube jutting from my stomach, along the insides of my legs. Everything she does is a connection to *me*. A deliberate and sensitive confluence. She looks so often into my eyes that it's impossible to imagine she can't see beyond the damaged layers and into my healthy soul, at a place where my muscles aren't atrophied from disuse, and where I can brush my own hair.

She talks to me. Snow-soft words. And again, hard to imagine that she can't feel my inner light shining. Not because of what she says, but how she says it. *You're doing so good, Wes.* Touching me deeply. Swirling. Drifting. *There . . . that feels better, huh?* The perfume of her hair as she leans close. Her breath, like a whisper, against my skin.

I talk to her, too, of course. Promises and daydreams. *I won't always be like this, Yvette. I'll be strong again. So strong.* All my hopes, gathered like children and sent to run wild. I know she can't hear me, but what's wrong with imagining she can? And there are moments when she will stop what she is doing and look at me, or smile and nod, as if she *can* hear me. I swear to God, when this happens, my heart jumps so hard that it makes my ribcage clatter.

As soon as I'm better, we'll go dancing. We'll—

I move more frequently when Yvette is with me. I'll push out my neck or roll my jaw. One time I raised my hand

and my fingertips brushed across her cheek. A random, unconscious movement, perhaps, but it reinforced that feeling of connection. Yvette took my hand, squeezed my fingers, and smiled. I floated for the rest of that day. Neither in nor out of my body. It was like dreaming.

In a normal relationship, two people get to know each other (primarily) through interaction. A privilege I cannot fully realize. The alternative is to follow her, like a private investigator, and so I do—more frequently than I should, but I'm helpless to resist. I have learned where she lives (a one-bedroom apartment on Lilywood Drive), what she listens to when she drives (CHUM FM), what she has for breakfast (vanilla yoghurt and a granola bar), the TV shows she has set to record on her PVR (too many to mention). I have browsed her books and DVD collection, listened to her talk on the phone, watched her workout at the gym, studied the way she interacts with her other patients (always kind, but—I'm *certain*—without the connection she has to me). All this and more, getting to know Yvette by violating her privacy. Not something I'm comfortable doing, but what choice do I have?

Obsessive? A smidge, perhaps. But I draw the line. Same as with Mom and Dad, I never jump into her mind, even though I'd love to know what she's thinking. I don't snoop through her underwear drawer or watch her in the shower. I use my superhero talent to discover only the things I would if I were able-bodied.

Believe me, I'd prefer a more traditional method of getting to know her. Talking, dating, and kissing. Gathering protons prior to collision. My process, while effective, lacks the personal touch. But that's what comes of being unseen, unheard. Although it is not without reward; I hovered over Yvette's shoulder while she Googled me, clicking on countless hits, reading about my surfing achievements and, of course, my accident. She brought up numerous pictures of me riding waves, or posing with my board, tanned and cut. I looked into her glittering eyes as she tried to collate the young athlete on her monitor with the broken man she was being paid to care for. Maybe she was Googling me out of curiosity, but I like to think it was because of the bond we had so quickly formed. We were, in a way, touching each other.

And just last weekend she was talking to her mom on Skype. I didn't realize Yvette was Québécoise until her mom's voice floated through the laptop's tiny speakers: "*Salut, Yvette. Comment va ma belle petite fille?*" I suppose her surname, Sommereux, should have given me some clue, but I had only ever heard her speaking English, even to herself, and was too preoccupied to register the accent.

"*Bonjour, Maman,*" she said, waving at the webcam. "*Ça va bien. Toi? Et Papa?*"

French was never my language. Had real difficulty with it in high school. But now, of course, I'm as fluent as Céline Dion.

"*Tout va bien ici, ma chérie. Mais tu nous manques tellement!*" Yvette's mom said, but what I heard was, "We're both well, sweetheart, but we miss you like crazy!"

"I miss you, too," Yvette said. Her smile was real, but touched with a wistfulness that pulled it down at the corners. Her eyes shone, though. As always. "I'm enjoying myself, but I do get lonely sometimes."

"You can always come home."

"I know, Mom."

The conversation was long, and I should probably have given Yvette some privacy and zipped out of there. But I couldn't. Not because I wanted to learn more about Yvette's life (although I did), or because I wanted to stay close to her (I did), but because I was feeding on the energy between Yvette and her mom. They were *conversing* and *laughing* and *loving*. Interaction that had been absent from my family for so long. I ached for it so much that tears gathered in the corners of my eyes. Even my useless body—in my groovy bedroom three and a half kilometres away—reacted: head rolling, legs twitching. It was *fuel* to me. I couldn't leave, even if I'd wanted to.

They talked about Yvette's father's angina medication, her younger sister's college application, the neighbour's new dog that barked every time a car drove by the house. More besides, and so much was mundane, yet threaded with the delightful uniqueness that defines a family. A way of laughing. An unfinished sentence. A certain word or phrase. Everything was loaded with love and understanding—something you only get when talking to someone with the same blood. So many people don't have this in their lives, but Yvette does. This makes me happy.

"So what's new and exciting with you?" Mrs. Sommereux asked as soon as she had finished recounting family affairs.

"I have a new patient," Yvette replied. "His name is Westlake Soul. Isn't that cute?"

I pricked up my ears and drifted a little closer.

"Westlake Soul," her mom said slowly, as if tasting the words. "Strange name. Is he black?"

"No, Mom," Yvette said, smiling. "He's a blond-haired,

blue-eyed surfer dude. Or at least he *used* to be a surfer dude. Now he's . . ." Her words faded as the corners of her smile dropped down again.

"He's . . . ?"

"It's just so sad," Yvette said, and proceeded to tell her mom about me. All of the things I have heard numerous times in the two years since my accident, and have come to expect: how I was once so handsome and strong, and how God can be inexplicably cruel—to cut me down in my prime, a young man with such *joie de vivre* (no translation necessary). She also said a few things that I didn't expect, and that nobody has said before. I wrapped myself around her, scarf-like, while my physical body jerked and leaked.

"He is like a cracked window that you have to wash so carefully, in case the pieces fall out." Yvette wasn't looking at her mom's face when she said this, but down at her keyboard, and I knew that I shimmered in her mind. Cracked, perhaps, but more likely tanned and cut. "Everybody thinks he is broken, but he is still intact. And sometimes, if you press your face to the glass, you can see through the cracks—"

"You shouldn't develop attachments to your patients, Yvette," Mrs. Sommereux said, frowning and motherly.

"Sometimes you can see *in*," Yvette continued, still looking at the keyboard. "It's very dark, but every now and then . . ."

Again, she trailed off. Lips turned down.

"Daddy is thinking about trading the Buick," Mrs. Sommereux said. Her image had frozen on the screen. A locked-in frown. As if the wind had changed direction. "He wants something a little sportier. Maybe a . . ."

Their conversation continued, and I stayed wrapped around Yvette. Didn't move until she shut down her computer and went to bed. I lay next to her as she drifted into sleep, stroking her hair, watching her small mouth move as she dreamed.

I need to get closer to her. Get to know her. There remains so much to discover. I have seen her flower, but not her roots. Only strength will show me more. Recovery. I need to be able to take her in my arms and share everything— touch her as deeply as she has touched me. And I *can* do it. I am more determined than ever to fix the cracks in my window, and to show her the light inside.

Yvette is twenty-four years old. Originally from Rouyn-Noranda, Québec. She has no pets. Only a plant that she talks to while she waters it. Her favourite singer is Alicia Keys. Her best friend's name is Heidi. She has a box of gymnastics trophies in her closet, and two framed diplomas that she has not hung up yet. She reads three pages—max—of a book before getting bored and putting it down. Two hundred and twelve Facebook friends. Her favourite colour is yellow. There's a picture of Johnny Depp in her wallet, behind her driver's licence. She can text approximately forty-five words per minute on her iPhone. She drinks peppermint tea.

Oh, and she has a boyfriend. His name is Wayne, and he is a fucktard of the first degree. More about Wayne later. But first, if you don't think that feeding Jevity 1.2 Cal formula through a percutaneous endoscopic gastrostomy tube can ever be sexy, check this out. . . .

10. Soul Food.

I haven't tasted food or drink for over two years. The last thing I drank was a glass of grapefruit juice before heading to the beach on that fateful morning in July of '09. The last thing I ate — food that passed down my throat and into my esophagus in the normal way—was a slice of cheese pizza. If I'd known it was going to be my final (real) meal, I would've gone for the meat-feast. Two slices.

In order for my body to receive the nutrients it needs to stay alive, I am fed through a pencil-thin polyurethane tube that passes through my abdominal wall and into my stomach. From here the food (a liquid formula) flows into my small intestine, and the nutrients are carried into my bloodstream. It's not pretty, but it works. Breakfast, lunch, dinner, and supper. Four meals a day poured directly into my stomach.

Yum.

I used to have an enteral feeding pump that administered formula and water as required. This eliminated the less-than-delightful method of bolus feeding, but—after finally being free of hospital machinery—Mom got upset when she saw me plugged into yet more gadgetry at home. She said it took away my humanness. So the pump was discarded after a few short weeks, and Mom and Dad learned how to bolus feed. It's not complicated, but needs to be done correctly to prevent infection, aspiration, and clogging of the tube. Mom will feed me at breakfast and dinner time. Dad gets the supper shift. They have it down to a fine art, and are usually in and out within fifteen minutes. They never complain, and the PVR means that they can do it without missing even a second of their favourite TV shows. (The gadgetry they are plugged into is obviously acceptable.)

My lunchtime feed always came courtesy of Fat Annie. Now, of course, this duty falls to Yvette.

The beginning of the week. Monday. I heard the yellow Beetle pull into our driveway and felt my body flush with excitement. The only evidence of this, however, was two dime-sized spots of colour on my cheeks. Hub started yapping—*She's here, Wes. Right outside. Just heard her car*—but she didn't come in right away. Impatiently, I streamed from my body and into the Beetle's passenger seat. Yvette was clutching her iPhone, jaw clenched, looking down at a text from Wayne the Fucktard. It read: UR LUCKY 2 HAVE ME BITCH I CN GET ANY PEICE OF ASS I WANT ANY TIME SO FUCK U. Yvette was debating how to respond. I touched her face and told her to ignore it, and she did. Pure coincidence, but it made me feel better, nonetheless. She shut off the phone, slotted it into one of the Beetle's cup holders, and came in to see me.

She wasn't herself. Her smile was strained, her eyes shaded. She still touched me with the same care, but barely spoke. I tried to think of some way I could reach her—assure her that everything would be okay—but I had nothing. (Some superhero, huh?) I had to settle for wrapping invisible arms around her, inhaling the fragrance of her coconut shampoo while wishing for her happiness to return. After my bed bath, she dressed me in fresh clothes and lifted me into my chair (not hard; lifting is all technique, and I'm not exactly heavy; I've dropped from a toned one-eighty to a near-transparent one-fifteen). It was fine outside, so she wheeled me onto the rear deck while she changed my bedsheets.

Hub came out and sat with me. We didn't talk. Just enjoyed the sunshine. It flashed high above us, a golden hole punched into the centre of the sky. The maples around our garden flaunted their leaves, like hands filled with coins. The sounds of our neighbourhood. Lawnmowers and insects. Children splashing in a pool. A radio playing summery jazz. Hub dozed, his fur shimmering. I sat in my chair and breathed.

Yvette came to get me just when I felt the right side of my face burning. I wished she'd slapped a little sunscreen on my cheeks, a floppy hat on my head, and left me out there for another hour or so. I was quite content, and the tranquility was refreshing. But she wheeled me back into the house, lifted me into bed, and then—amazingly—stroked my face where it had reddened in the sun. So tender, like a lover.

"I left you out there too long," she said. "I'm sorry, Wes."

I looked at her. A tiny vein in my left eyelid ticked. I imagined how the curve of her spine would feel against my palm. My hips pressed against her stomach. My other hand on her thigh, tracing the line of her underwear through a gauzy skirt painted with flowers.

Her fingers moved from my cheek to my hair. Tousling and gently tugging. Dark blond at the roots. White at the tips.

"Sweet Wes," she said.

I sighed and my lips turned upward. Almost a smile.

Everybody thinks he is broken, but he is still intact, Yvette had said to her mother. *And sometimes, if you press your face to the glass, you can see through the cracks—*

She was doing it now. Looking through the cracks. My heart roared.

Sometimes you can see in.

I gave her the sun. Everything in my soul—wanting her to not just see my light, but *feel* it. A solar flare that would suck all the oxygen from the room and leave us both breathless. Her thumb brushed the corner of my eye, where a tear had gathered. Her lips parted and for one magnificent moment (not nearly long enough) I thought she was going to kiss me. Instead she removed her hand from my face and stood up quickly. The slightest frown touched her brow and she gave her head a little shake.

I trembled. Sighed again.

Yvette stepped away from my bed and shuffled, in a somewhat distracted manner, to Westlake's Wall of Achievement, where my surfing trophies are loaded onto shelves, and pictures of me in healthier, happier days hang in funky glass frames. Her back to me, she looked at the pictures (the glass *not* cracked) for a long time. I slipped from my body and floated by her side, wanting—*needing*— to see her expression. I watched as she reached up and touched one of the pictures. One of my favourite shots: shooting the curl at Banzai Pipeline. She didn't touch the aquamarine wave, or the pale strip of sky above it. She touched *me*. Her fingertip followed the lines of my body, from my wet hair to where my toes clutched the board. Then she moved to the next picture—the one of me with Patrick Swayze. It was taken at the US Open in 2006. A close-up of our faces. High cheekbones, shining eyes, brilliant smiles. Neither of us aware of the darkness in our future. Yvette touched this picture, too. My face, but not Patrick Swayze's. She ran her finger along my smile, then turned to look at me in the bed. From one version of Westlake to another. That frown again.

"*Je trouve l'existence incompréhensible,*" she said. The first time she had spoken French—knowingly—in my presence.

I don't understand life, either, I replied. *And I'm the smartest dude in the world.*

"*C'est cruel.*"

Yes, I agreed. *So cruel.*

She turned to the regiment of trophies, standing to attention, glimmering in the early afternoon light. Seven in total, and three medals, hanging from their ribbons, die-cast exclamation marks. She read every engraved nameplate. Touched the polished pedestals and figures. She *caressed* my Billabong Classic trophy—curled her hand around the column and slipped it up and down. Ran the tip of her thumb over the happy little surfer dude on top. I could be wrong, but I think she did this because she wanted to connect—on a psychometric level—to the former me. The trophies were solid and unchanged. As real now as they were when I won them. They could easily be my muscles or square shoulders. My firm jaw or the healthy part of my brain. My happiness . . .

"*C'est cruel.*"

I flowed back into my body and huddled, feeling the deep pain of loss. That vein in my eyelid still ticked. I groaned and Yvette turned to face me.

"Sweet Wes," she said. English again, and I watched as she reached back and pulled the band from her hair. Light brown hair tumbled across one side of her face. She took a step toward me. Her lips were wet.

Beneath the sheets, my legs began to sweat.

"It's lunchtime," she said. "You must be so . . ." She paused, took another step toward me, bit her lower lip, and finished: "Hungry."

The vein in my eyelid ticked quicker still.

She smiled, brushed the hair from her face (it fell back almost immediately), and started to assemble the necessary supplies: a hand towel, a pitcher of tap water, two empty glasses, a stethoscope, a tin of my prescribed formula, a catheter tip syringe. She placed everything on a folding table beside my bed, smiling deliciously, partially obscured by that veil of hair. I followed her with my eyes, feeling (bizarrely) like I had when I was seventeen and about to lose my virginity. Rigid with nervous energy. My heart somewhere in my throat, restricting respiration. Anticipation like a 747 taking to the sky.

Yvette pulled back the sheets, revealing my body. Legs flopped sideways and toes curled. My T-shirt had rucked up a little, offering a glimpse of my abdomen and the strip of pale hair that runs from my bellybutton to my groin (my Treasure Trail—that's what Nadia called it). Yvette sanitized her hands with a squirt of Purell. The clear liquid glistened between her fingers, making wet sounds as she rubbed it in. Another dazzling smile, then she reached down and lifted my T-shirt up to my chest. I felt her fingernails drag lightly over my skin.

"Let's take care of you, Wes," she said, but what my spinning mind heard was, *Gonna take real good care of you, baby.*

She put on the stethoscope and placed the chestpiece on my abdomen, leaning closer as she listened for irregular sounds. Her long hair brushed across my face. I inhaled deeply and imagined some coconut-littered paradise, reclining on a bed of husks as Yvette—her lips cold from the ocean—kissed my stomach. This little fantasy faded when she took the stethoscope away, but I didn't mind. She touched me. So gently. Three fingers pressing my abdomen with exquisite care, feeling for bumps or swelling. Anything . . . distended. Satisfied, she slowly drew back her hand, raking one fingernail through the Treasure Trail, and raised the head of my bed to a sixty-degree angle. I felt the machinery vibrate through my body . . . bones trembling happily as I rose to a more upright position. Yvette nodded, flipped the hair from her eyes, and poured appropriate measures of formula and water into the two glasses. I waited, a little breathless, moisture leaking from the corner of my mouth.

She snapped on a pair of latex gloves and I watched her upper lip curl. Both mischievous and enticing.

"Don't want you getting all messy," she said, placing the hand towel on my stomach to catch potential spillage. Then she took my tube in hand, assessing its length, sliding her fingers up and down and tugging expertly, ensuring a clean connection. My eyes fluttered and I moaned. I wondered if her heart was drumming as passionately as mine—if we were feeling the same emotion: a strong hand that cradled us delicately, and lifted us to a place where the air smelled of sugarcane and the birds were multicoloured. I drifted there for a while, sensation coursing through me as if barrels of desire had been tipped over deep inside. When I came back Yvette had slipped the syringe's catheter tip into the end of my tube, pushing it in nice and tight. She moistened her lips and administered the primary flush— thirty millilitres of water poured into the syringe, flowing through the tube and into my stomach. I felt it dripping inside me, cool and satisfying.

Feels so good, I said. My chin was slick with drool and beads of sweat glistened on the bridge of my nose.

Next came my formula. Fifty millilitres of Jevity 1.2 Cal, loaded with protein and calories to keep me from wasting away to bones. With a steady hand Yvette poured it into the barrel of the syringe, not wasting one drop. I groaned again and Yvette smiled.

"You like that, huh?"

Feels so good.

She moved her hand up and down, raising and lowering the syringe, controlling how quickly the formula flowed into my stomach. My fingertips tingled and my left leg stretched out, shaking, toes still curled.

You're . . . amazing.

"Almost there, Wes."

Eyelid still flickering, I stared at her while she finished off—at that sheaf of hair, the set of her mouth, and the splash of colour that had risen from beneath the collar of her blouse. I longed to touch her there, in those bright, pink places, but all I could do was stare. The last drop of formula rolled down the tube and into my stomach, and she followed it with the secondary flush. More water. Cool and strangely refreshing. I imagined kissing the sweat from the shallow pockets beneath her eyes. Licking the taste from my lips.

Yvette removed the syringe and plugged the adapter.

"We're all done," she said.

Tingling throughout my body. Toes uncurling.

Amazing, I said again.

My head rolled on its loose hinge, facing away from Yvette now, but that was okay. I sighed and listened to my heartbeat. Proof of life, and of feeling. Sunlight poured through the window and I watched Yvette's shadow—as unlikely and thin as my body—flicker against the wall as she cleaned up. Hypnotic movement that lured me into sleep. When I awoke the sunlight had shifted but Yvette was still there, rubbing calamine lotion into my reddened cheek. I willed my eyes to close so that I couldn't see my crippled body, or the Wall of Achievement that reminded me so often of what I had lost. I thought—with eyes closed and Yvette stroking my face—that for just one moment I could feel normal. Wasn't to be, though. I looked at my trophies, and at the photo of me and Patrick Swayze grinning unknowingly.

So I released. Again. My version of running away, refusing to face reality. I flew in wild circles, venting passion and rage, and by the time I returned Yvette had gone home, the sun had dropped into a pool of red colour, and the vein in my left eyelid had finally stopped ticking.

11. The Bad Guys.

There is no warning. No sudden cold feeling. One moment life is bopping along as always (bizarre but steady), and the next I am fighting Dr. Quietus, wondering if the next breath will be my last. He came for me Tuesday morning—the day after Yvette let down her hair and bolus fed me like I'd never been bolus fed before. 07:13 AM. I'd just woken up, staring at the ceiling while the pain of sleeping in one position eased from my muscles. I could smell toast and coffee. Dad was getting ready for work. Mom was half asleep, one hand on the alarm clock, ready to hit the snooze button the moment it started beeping. Niki and Hub were curled up on the same bed, equally lost to their dreams. Outside my window, nature turned its reliable face toward the sun, while commuters busied roads, sidewalks, and drive-thrus. Wings of mist lifted from the fields surrounding Hallow Falls. Trains shook their rails en route to the city. Early flights out of Lester B. Pearson marked a sky the colour of new eyes.

Just another morning in the Golden Horseshoe.

Dr. Quietus wrapped his hands around my throat and

jerked me from this world so hard that my body didn't even move. Galileo's concept of inertia at work. Kind of like that old trick of pulling away a tablecloth and leaving everything standing. Morning light—everything natural—disappeared, along with the smell of coffee and toast. He threw me onto the roof of a burning tower. I landed hard, spitting blood. Through columns of black smoke I saw him move toward me. Sometimes he walks upright and tall, almost human. Sometimes he is on all fours, his muscles moving liquidly beneath his skin and his deathly head low to the ground. Now he *skulked*, somewhere between the two, his mysterious face hidden in the shadows of his cowl.

Did you miss me? he asked.

Dr. Quietus can't be defeated. The best I can do is keep him at bay. When he comes back, he's always a little stronger than the time before. One day, obviously—same for us all—he'll be too powerful. This wasn't going to be that day. I was *determined*. Yvette Sommereux had just flowed into my life and, amazingly, we were connecting. My family was in turmoil. They needed me. It was not a good time to lose everything.

And so, as always, I fought.

If you think I'm just going to roll over, I said. *Think again*.

He flew at me and I burst left, through a curtain of flame, but he was quicker—wrapped one arm around my waist and pulled me close. His breath crawled over my face and throat. I thrashed and managed to get away, then ran across the crumbling roof and threw myself over the edge. I didn't fall; I soared, and with altitude saw that it was not just the building I'd leapt from, but the whole city in flames.

Trees and billboards. Roads and walkways. I watched a bridge collapse in a riot of burning pieces. Buildings—from bungalows to skyscrapers—crumpled and exhaled great mushrooms of smoke and fire. Everything was coming apart.

What's going on here? I said. Usually, when I battle Dr. Quietus, I set the scene. It is, after all, my life—my fight to lose. But this was all wrong. A feeling of helplessness slowed me down. Was I losing control? Or was control being stripped away? Both possibilities filled me with dread.

I stopped flying.

I fell.

It's coming apart around you, Westlake. Dr. Quietus bolted after me, so quick and strong, and so dark it was difficult to distinguish him from the rising smoke. *Piece by piece, and there's nothing you can do about it.*

I hit the ground hard.

THWAAMM!

Smouldering debris. Flames like threatened snakes. A nearby structure collapsed with a deafening roar, throwing a pocket of heat that flipped me onto my back. I lay there, searching the sky for a seam of light—my escape—but all I could see was smoke, lit from within by the glow of the flames.

Dr. Quietus touched down beside me. He laughed coarsely, then dragged me to my feet.

It's all too easy, he snarled. *All the hard work is being done for me. Can't you see that?*

I hung from one of his fists like a wet jacket. So close to his face—monstrous breath, spitting embers—but I caught only a glimpse. His sharp mouth. One diseased eye. I reached up and clasped his arm. The flexed muscle reminded me of the trains I had seen shaking their way into the city only moments before.

Not so smart, after all.

Sparks drowned my eyes. He drove his other fist into my stomach and threw me aside. I tumbled through the ruin like a hat in the wind—crashed through a burning wall and into a room I recognized at once. My old bedroom in the house I grew up in. We'd lived there until I was fifteen years old. I knew it as well as I knew the groovy room. The furniture was in flames but it was all there. My crazy-cool loft bed with the Godzilla comforter. My little desk with the computer on top, next to my collection of Toronto Blue Jays bobbleheads (I watched as the monitor exploded and Carlos Delgado melted into a creamy puddle of goop). My bookcase with its haphazard arrangement of books and comics. *Chicka Chicka Boom Boom* and *Where the Wild Things Are* and *Maniac Magee*. So many more, stacked until the shelves were sighing, but all in flames now, their spines buckled and peeling. And, of course, there was Westlake's Wall of Achievement, version #1, adorned with paintings and crafts, certificates and badges, and two small trophies. One for hockey, the other for skateboarding. Flames licked across the wall and the corners of the paintings curled and blackened. I leapt to my feet, crying out, forgetting Dr. Quietus for the moment and trying to rescue the mementos of my early life. I plucked the certificates from the wall and quelled the flames with my bare hands. I grabbed ugly pottery, daubed permanently with my little thumbprints, only to have it crumble between my fingers and fall in dull shards to the ground. A painting of planet earth (WESTLAKE SOUL AGE 7 scrawled in one corner) began to blister—broad brown holes—as if it were being struck by asteroids. I snatched it down and blew on the spreading flames, but it only quickened the destruction. Within seconds it was engulfed. Clumps of ash rained down on my dandy superhero boots.

It's the end of the world, Westlake, Dr. Quietus said, stepping over glowing rubble and timbers burned to a velvety texture. *The end of your world, at least.*

I looked at him, emerging from flames, his shadow dancing everywhere. Smoke rippled from beneath his cowl. I imagined him exhaling it from lungs like bullet casings.

It's all over, he said.

My helpless feeling deepened. I sagged, fell against the wall. Watched my Godzilla comforter go up in flames. My computer keyboard buckle. My bookcase collapse and spit a mouthful of charred pieces, like crows flying into a fan. Dr. Quietus laughed as my hockey trophy hit the floor and broke into three burning pieces. I caught my skateboarding trophy before it could do the same. The column was scorched. Too hot to hold, but I held it, anyway—*gripped* it. The figure had melted. No longer a silver-toned dude pulling a handplant. More like a stiletto heel, or a spearhead with the tip snipped off.

There's no escape this time, Dr. Quietus growled.

I thought of Dad, drinking coffee and brushing toast crumbs off his tie, unaware that his only son was dying in the bedroom down the hall. And Mom, one hand on the alarm clock, dreaming hazily while her firstborn breathed his last.

It's over, Westlake.

Niki and Hub sleeping, curled together like a couple of horseshoes. My body would be a waxen shell by the time they woke up. As lifeless as the tube jutting from my stomach.

More smoke oozed from Dr. Quietus's grin. He took another step toward me.

And Yvette . . . I thought of her, too. Hair covering one side of her face. Looking through my cracked window.

I pushed myself off the wall and squared my shoulders.

No, I said. *There's too much to live for. People who love me. Need me.* I thought of the ocean. Pink and blue and orange and white. Roaring and breaking. *Too many waves yet to ride . . . to tame.*

Dr. Quietus faltered. His grin disappeared.

It's not your choice, he said.

My life. My choice.

Not anymore.

He growled and ran at me, lowering his shoulders and swinging fists the size of warheads. His cloak flapped as he leapt a pile of burning debris, and I cocked my right arm, drawing the skateboarding trophy over my shoulder. I threw it as his boots clunked down, less than ten feet away. It whizzed through the air like a giant dart, flames flickering from the base, and struck him square in the middle of the chest.

SHHWUUMPP!

A scream—more smoke—bellowed from inside the cowl. Dr. Quietus staggered back. He grasped the part of the trophy that protruded from his chest and dislodged it with a sucking sound. I used the moment to strike again, kicking up a swirl of distracting ashes, then lunging forward and ramming my fist into the mysterious bone of his face.

KA-THUNK!

He turned a full three-sixty, toppled backward, and crashed into the utility space beneath my loft bed. Two of the posts crumbled and the bed—still burning—collapsed on top of him. An umbrella of sparks and ashes opened, marking my departure like a magician's smoke effect. I launched myself though the damaged roof and into the sky. Going up . . . only up. I didn't look down until the ruin was no bigger than my thumbnail.

The air cleared.

I found the seam. Opened my eyes.

I'd been gone for almost six hours. It felt more like fifteen minutes. Mom and Niki were arguing in the kitchen. Something about a cell phone bill. Hub was sneering at blackbirds in the back garden. Yvette had been and gone. I lay against the pillows, staring at my toes, perfectly still but shaking inside.

I recalled the painting of planet earth that I had done—and been so proud of—when I was seven years old. Burning in my hands.

It's the end of the world, Westlake, Dr. Quietus had said.

No.

I tried to shake my head. Couldn't.

In a moment I was gone again. Not battling Dr. Quietus, or releasing to some heavenly locale, but surfing the universal wave function. It flowed and twisted through my history, and with every trick I pulled—every door thrown open and memory seized—it collapsed and threw me back into the core stream. Imagine riding an escalator and stepping off at the top, wanting to head left or right into this or that department, only to have the ground move beneath your feet and whip you upward again. The inexorable passage of fate—*my* fate—but I twisted and kicked against it. Didn't *WANT* it. A barracuda fighting on the line. A falling man trying to flip gravity. Yet an unkind truth occurred to me: if I *were* to find a branch point, and assume an alternate life, I would lose Yvette forever. She wouldn't even figure in my thoughts. And it's not like I could track her down and make her mine, because an alternate Westlake would have no knowledge of her existence. It was a no-brainer, of course—you can't miss what you've never had—but still upsetting. I slowed down, flopped my face into my hands, then screamed at a billion closed doors.

My throat was burning by the time I slipped back into my fractured shell. It was nighttime. Everybody sleeping. The house ticked like a rheumatic joint. My eyes were wide in the darkness. A muscle in my thigh thumped weakly.

It's coming apart around you, Westlake.

There has to be a way out of this.

Piece by piece, and there's nothing you can do about it.

Fuck Dr. Quietus. Fuck death.

It's all over.

I'm not giving up.

The house groaned in reply. I stared at nothing, too shaken up to sleep, and so released. I found kindness and passion and love. Qualities to counteract doom. I absorbed them, and felt their benefit. Soon my throat had stopped burning, and I submarined into the ocean and swam with bioluminescent creatures—drawn like constellations— that latched onto my back like insect wings.

Or maybe I dreamed that last part. Hard to say. The next thing I knew it was morning. I could smell coffee and toast again.

Calmer. The sun pressing through the blinds. My family—although preoccupied with their own affairs—around me. I talked to Hub for a while, but didn't tell him about Dr. Quietus. Didn't want to worry the dude. Afterward, he jumped onto my bed and slept the way dogs sometimes do: four paws in the air, little teeth showing. Listening to him snore made me feel drowsy, too. I caught patchy but pleasant sleep, and was woken fully by the telephone ringing. It was Yvette. She was feeling under the weather and wouldn't be coming in. Mom screwed her eyes shut and gritted her teeth, but said it was fine and to get better soon. I heard Yvette's voice buzzing through the earpiece. She said she was sorry. I could tell she had been crying. Mom hung up, swore colourfully, and then called her part-time job to tell them that—so sorry—something had come up and she couldn't make it in. The voice at the other end of the line snapped more than buzzed.

Mom was pissed off. She was bound to catch flak from her boss, and for something beyond her control. I was more upset, though. I had wanted—*needed*—to see Yvette. Her care, and her touch, would be so healing after my recent clash with Dr. Quietus. I left Hub with his paws up and flew to her apartment on Lilywood Drive. She was huddled on the sofa, dressed in Winnie the Pooh pyjamas. Alicia Keys playing on the stereo. Crumpled Kleenex on the floor. Her face was wet with tears and, yes, she looked under the weather. A touch of flu, perhaps. Then she turned her head to the side and I saw the bruise beneath her left eye.

And so we come to Wayne the Fucktard.

Ripped. Head shaved. A maple leaf tattooed on each arm. The first time I saw him, he pulled up outside Yvette's apartment in a big-ass pickup truck, a toolbox in the bed and his company's name—APPETITE FOR CONSTRUCTION—stencilled on the doors. I'd been chilling with Yvette, sharing the sofa with her as she watched Dr. Oz. She buzzed him up. "Hey, baby," she said at the door, and leaned forward for a kiss, but he brushed past her and clomped into the kitchen in his dusty workman's boots. "I just vacuumed," she said. Wayne rolled green eyes that were set a little too close together (a sign of untrustworthiness, according to the ancient Greeks, and you'll get no argument from me), opened the fridge and helped himself to a beer. Yvette looked at the arcs of dirt left in the carpet as he stomped into the living room. He took no notice of her. Gulped his beer, dropped his ass onto the sofa next to me, and flicked the TV over to Sportsnet.

I've told you very little about Wayne, but I'm willing to bet you've a fairly accurate picture of him in your head. The kind of guy who has Kimbo Slice wallpaper on his cell phone, and who thinks *The Expendables* should have won ten Academy Awards.

This is your boyfriend? I said to Yvette, who was still looking at the dirt arcs in the carpet. We both wore mystified, somewhat hurt expressions. *What are you thinking?* I didn't stick around for an answer. I flipped back into my body and pondered the age-old anomaly of beautiful, intelligent girls dating total asswipes.

Jealous? Yeah, a little. But if Wayne was a good dude, I'd

at least be jealous *and* happy for her. He's not a good dude, though. He's a fucktard.

The second time I saw him was even worse.

They'd been out on a date (by which I mean, Wayne had watched UFC at Boston Pizza, while Yvette sat next to him, playing Angry Birds on her iPhone). He drank too many beers but drove home anyway—told Yvette to shut her fucking cakehole when she offered to drive. They got back to Yvette's place and he came on strong. She pushed him away and told him that she wasn't in the mood. "The fuck you're not," Wayne said. He wrapped his hand around her throat and squeezed. "I just bought you fucking pizza. New York Cheesecake, too." I raged and swung invisible fists at him, wishing they had substance, wishing he could feel *something*. But I couldn't even disturb the air. Yvette managed to squirm out of his grasp. She stood in the middle of the room and shook her head. The shape of Wayne's hand was imprinted on her throat. I continued to throw empty punches at him. "You've had too much to drink," she said. "You can sleep on the sofa or go home." He growled and stepped toward her, one fist raised, knuckles scuffed. She said, "Please no," and backed away and he grinned, lowered his fist, told her she was a lousy lay and that he'd rather jack off, anyway. I stopped swinging haymakers and tried the *Scanners* thing, but his head remained, regrettably, intact. I tried the *Carrie* thing, too—mining the iceberg for telekinetic ability, wanting to open the kitchen drawers and fling knives at him. Forks, too. I'd bounce the toaster off his head for good measure. It was a weighty appliance with four slots and a bagel function. It would hurt like a bastard. Couldn't do it, though. And couldn't do the *Firestarter* thing, either. I just stood there, frustrated as hell, feeling like the most useless superhero since Aquaman.

"Bitch," Wayne said. He spat on the carpet, then turned to leave. Our eyes locked for half a second. They seemed to, at least, but then he walked right through me . . . and I *felt* him, I swear to God. His anger and insecurity. His unkindness. It gathered inside me, brick-heavy. A block of poison. I stumbled—my floaty *soul* stumbled—while back in the groovy room my shell moaned and curled a fist. Then he was gone, slamming the door so hard the blinds jumped in the windows and a waft of hall-smelling air blew the hair back from Yvette's face. I went to her. Held her ineffectually. Followed her into the bedroom as she threw her face into the pillows and cried.

The next morning—Monday—she sent him a text: LAST NIGHT WASN'T GOOD. LET'S TRY AGAIN TONIGHT. IF U CAN BE KIND, I COULD BE "IN THE MOOD" ;-) XOXOXO And that was when he texted her back, her iPhone jingling as she pulled into my driveway: UR LUCKY 2 HAVE ME BITCH I CN GET ANY PEICE OF ASS I WANT ANY TIME SO FUCK U. So she came in and touched my trophies and pulled the band from her hair and cared for me, and for a long, sweet moment forgot all about Wayne the Fucktard.

Je trouve l'existence incompréhensible.

Those crumpled Kleenex, like the snipped heads of lilies. Alicia Keys singing, "Fallin'." That crescent of purple skin beneath her left eye.

It happened while I was away—either looking for a branch point or swimming with glowing lobates—but I have been able to piece together events from telephone conversations and text messages. Not that I *needed* to piece together events. Yvette didn't walk into a door or fall down the stairs. Wayne hit her. He *punched* her. One of those ugly fists connected with the delicate structure of her cheekbone hard enough to rupture tiny veins and capillaries. I knew this as soon as I saw her. Learning that Wayne had been drunk at the time, and that they'd had a thunderous argument, changed nothing. It didn't heal the contusion. It didn't rewind time and make everything right. The son of a bitch *hit* her. Nothing else mattered.

I went to her, and held her in my special way. We listened to Alicia, wrapped together. Fragile, yet strong. Her heartbeat bounced through my soul like light in a house of mirrors. She crumpled Kleenex while I considered my own source of woe: Dr. Quietus, gliding like a hawk, just waiting to strike. Then I thought of the Joker and the Penguin, Lex Luthor and Doomsday, the Green Goblin and Venom.

And now, of course, Wayne Hubbins, AKA Wayne the Fucktard.

So many supervillains. Not enough heroes.

I stroked Yvette's face. Kissed the bruise beneath her eye.

He'll pay for hurting you, I said.

And he will. I'm not sure how yet, but one way or another—from the grip of this vegetative condition—I'm going to kick that bad guy's ass.

It's what superheroes do.

12. ?!?!?!

Still the box has not stopped rolling. My hands, my hands. Clay and plastic. Sometimes all I can move. Expressions cast in the flexing of fingers, the twist of a thumb. Some desperate language. While inside, the train puffs on tracks once edge-straight, now hook-crooked. Toward—*choo-choo!*—a bridge they never finished building. A bridge blown to nothing by bandits with faces like pearls. Outside the world pulsates. Green no more. A hateful, purple mouth. An open heart. I release through skin and smoke. Scream all the way nowhere. And disbelief hangs above me, as light as a balloon. Bopping with laughter against a ceiling painted Surf City Blue.

13. Respite.

I need some time alone. Need to think this through. Really, I'm too stunned to do anything more than float right now. If you could see my soul, it would be hovering above my body. Shimmering, like polished bone. Attached by threads that break too easily, too quickly. Guitar strings made of cobweb. So I need to find a place—inside me, probably. A central place where I can unfloat. I want to scream and run at the walls. I want to cry for understanding.

This world hurts my eyes. My heart.

I'm not sure when I'll be back.

Or for how long.

14. Why Fat Annie Quit.

You're all laughing at me. I just know it. All this time I've been telling you how smart I am—how I flipped the iceberg and can bury Stephen Hawking. Goethe, too. *The most powerful mind on the planet*, I said. *I'm a superhero. I can talk to dogs and astral project. Swim with whales. Think in five thousand languages.* Yeah, maybe in my own rotten apple of a brain. But I'm obviously not smart enough to *think* my way out of this permanent vegetative state. Or even to read the writing on the wall.

The clues were there, baby. They were there all along.

Fat Annie quitting, out of the blue. The heavy vibe. The solemnity and silence. Hub—all but forgotten in this fog of misery—not being taken for a walk. *The atmosphere in the house has been shitty*, he'd said. *And I for one don't dig it.*

Dad crying as the rain fell outside, his face in my lap. Everything grey. *We love you, Wes. You know that, right?*

And Mom, too. All those tears. *What do you want, Westlake?* So much tension between her and Dad. I thought maybe they were surfing the marital heavies. It happens, right?

And then there was the way he'd snapped at her when they were loading the dishwasher. *What's the point, anyway?* Talking about interviewing a new caregiver, and Mom had replied, *I haven't decided anything.* So many clues. So much writing on the wall. Impossibly large letters. All bright colours. Jesus Christ, I was so blind. So *stupid.* I bet even Darryl figured it out, behind the wheel of his green Camaro, Lady Gaga shooting from the speakers. *But things will get easier?* Turning it into a question by lifting the last word, and Dad had looked out the window. *Not before they get a lot harder,* he'd said.

Some superbrain, huh?

I feel so sick.

And I'm scared. *So* scared.

They're ending my life support. They're doing it. Really doing it. They're going to remove my feeding tube and starve me to death.

I still don't quite believe it . . . and it's because of this naïveté that I failed to see it in the first place. I never thought—not for one second—that my family could even *consider* such a thing. They love me, right? *Right?* Any other explanation for the shitty vibe seemed more plausible. Divorce. Erectile dysfunction. Fucking alien invasion. Dumb trust, on my part, and even dumber love. I'm like the dog that jumps into the back seat of the car, thinking— all excitedly—that he's going for the king of walks. Maybe chase some birds or swim in the river. Tail flapping and head out the window, tongue like a windsock. When all the time he's on his way to the vet's office. A quick shot of Euthanyl and no more walkies. Not ever. Only difference . . . it won't be quick for me. It could take weeks for me to die.

Fuck.

I can't let them do it.

I'll jump into their minds. I don't care about their secrets. Their privacy. I'll hammer against their walls until they hear me. What else can I do? Just let it happen? Just give in and die?

Not this kid.

I found out . . . Jesus, I can't even remember. Three days ago? Five? That's how scrambled my brain is. Anyway, I found out. And the only reason I did was that Mom told Yvette—called her into the living room for a meeting. At first I didn't grasp it. Or I refused to grasp it, more like. See . . . even then, hearing Mom articulate the words, it still wouldn't compute. Perfect denial or perfect stupidity. It amounts to the same thing.

I was on the rear deck with Hub, parked in the shade. A couple of dudes enjoying the fresh air. But Hub suddenly jerked up, ears cocked and eyes wide. It was how he sometimes looked when Mom and Dad played *Just Dance* on the Wii.

Jesus Christ, he said.

What? I said.

Seriously, Wes, didn't you hear that?

Maybe . . . I'm not sure, I just . . . But of course I heard. The back door was wide open. The windows, too. It was so still outside that I could hear everything inside. The clock in the hallway ticking, the radio turned down low, even the refrigerator humming. So yeah, I heard Mom talking to Yvette. Loud and clear. *Something about . . . I think . . .* Information barely computed, discarded with dumb and trustful abandon. My head out the window, in other words.

Tongue like a windsock. *Yeah, it was—*

Mom just said that they're going to remove your feeding tube.

Oh, I said, and snapped out of my body. A reflex action. A cobra extending its hood. I floated, trembled. Imagined myself: heat haze.

A couple of weeks had passed since the incident with Wayne the Fucktard, and I'd spent most of that time with Yvette. Throwing comfort vibes at her, trying to resonate with her biofield. I also spent hours—maybe even days—thinking of ways I could get back at Wayne. The bruise beneath Yvette's eye gradually faded, but my anger didn't. Thusly engaged, I missed what was happening back at the homestead: Dad and Mom discussing the issue of removing my feeding tube in depth, and then involving Niki in their conversation (she tore from the room, slammed her bedroom door—cried for six hours). I missed them surfing through countless stories on the Internet about families who had made the excruciating decision to discontinue life support for a loved one, and in each case saying they would do it again, that they had made the right decision. They had two meetings with the doctor. Not Dr. Thinker, but a youngish dude who looked like the guy who played Harvey Dent in *The Dark Knight*. The first meeting was to see what was involved. The second to see when it could be done. They arranged counselling sessions. For Niki, too. Apparently, killing a family member is a traumatic experience. Who'd've thunk it?

No. Wait. They're doing this because they *love* me.

They love me.

"It's what Westlake would want," Mom told Yvette.

Hub ran to the bottom of the garden and whined.

I flexed and shimmered. Stretched out. The sky beckoned, so clean and open, and the temptation to soar into it—high enough to punch a hole through its thin blue skin was overwhelming. I stayed close to my body, though. Close to Mom and Yvette. And to Hub, his ears flattened, paws covering his eyes.

"You've obviously given this a great deal of thought?" Yvette said. I couldn't tell if it was a question or not, but I like to think it was.

"Until we could feel our heads splitting under the pressure," Mom said. "It's not a decision we arrived at lightly."

"Of course," Yvette said.

"It's been awful," Mom said. "The most difficult, heartbreaking decision we've ever had to make. Constant turmoil. Constant doubt. Long periods of hating ourselves. And each other. It's been . . ."

Her lips moved for a while but no sound came out. She tried to hold back the tears but couldn't. Yvette went to her, perched on the arm of the chair, one hand on her shoulder. A gentle squeeze. I cried also, but nobody saw. I screamed. Nobody heard.

"We've been in contact with people who have been through the same ordeal," Mom continued, smearing her cheeks with the heels of her hands. "E-mails and telephone calls. Trying to gain some perspective. We've had second and third opinions—spoken to specialists and explored possible treatments, from deep brain stimulation to so-called miracle drugs. But in each case the doctors have assured us that the damage to Westlake's brain is too advanced. Nothing can be done."

Yvette grabbed the Kleenex from the kitchen counter. The box was peach and baby blue. It had flowers on it, and a butterfly. Mom plucked at one but two came out, as if the clever little tissues knew that one would not be enough. They were right.

"I can't tell you how many times I've prayed to a God I don't believe in, or how many wishes I've spent on first stars and fallen eyelashes."

Mom has become adept—not to mention eco-friendly— at getting the absolute most out of a single Kleenex. She will fold it into a firm rectangular pad, then dab until the surface is sodden, turn it over, dab again, unfold, refold, dab . . . and repeat until every square millimetre of the tissue is wet.

"Two years since the accident," she said, folding and dabbing. "We thought it would get easier, but it's only gotten harder. And for the longest time we held on to the fantasy that Westlake would recover. You read about miracles sometimes, don't you?"

Yvette nodded and squeezed Mom's shoulder.

"But that won't happen. God doesn't exist, and wishing is for dreamers. Nothing can bring Westlake back, and it's tearing us apart. With nowhere to turn we've had to face facts, look each other in the eye, and answer one simple question . . ."

Dab and unfold.

"What would Westlake want?"

I jumped from my body and wrapped myself around Yvette, hoping she would absorb me the way the Kleenex absorbed Mom's tears. *This is where you tell her about the cracked window,* I wailed. *Tell her how you can sometimes see* in . . . *that there's a light inside.*

Yvette looked at the floor, where the shadow of a bumblebee danced in a sun-puddle. Her lips were pressed so firmly together I couldn't see the join.

Save me, Yvette. Tell her that we CONNECT.

She said nothing.

Desperate, without alternative, I leapt into her mind. Chaos in there. A wild array of data, growing bright and then fading. Swirling and separating. I tried to convert it into images—see it in my mind the way Yvette saw it in hers. This is nothing like the psychics you see on TV, who hook thoughts like they are hooking rubber duckies in a carnival game. It's more like downloading. Processing binary code. I stole incomplete imagery that meant nothing to me: the front of a building I didn't recognize; water lapping against the stern of a corn-yellow boat; the hem of a summer dress. Scattered thoughts, possibly triggered by the sun-puddle, maybe the bumblebee. I saw myself, too. My legs like kindling. My hair one shade too dark. I hacked into this image before it could fade away, found another complex string of binary, and converted it. A vibration this time—a *feeling*, rather than a thought. Impossible to accurately represent in words. That would be like trying to count the facets of a snowflake at one glance. To expound the analogy: snowflake = fluffy, feeling = doubt. In other words, I knew that Yvette was resonating with that connection, that light inside, and she wasn't sure that ending life support was the right thing to do.

TELL HER! I screamed. *Please, Yvette.*

But she didn't. For all her admirable qualities, there remains a broad strip of insecurity. I'd seen it with Wayne the Fucktard. Constantly doubting herself, apologizing when she didn't have to, and taking him back when she should have known better. I pushed deeper into her mind, faced the blockade of her conscious, and willed her to bypass all insecurities— to challenge Mom's assessment of what was best for me.

I hammered on that wall until I was weary.

Hub howled in the garden. Ears still flattened.

Fold and dab.

"He used to be so active," Mom said. "Always, and from such a young age. He was walking at eight months. *Eight*. My sister couldn't believe it. We just knew he'd be an athlete someday. All those trophies and medals . . ."

"Yes, I've seen them," Yvette said.

"You've seen *some* of them," Mom said. "There are more in the basement. Three boxes more."

She started on the second Kleenex. I pulled myself from Yvette's mind and sagged in the air. I always felt so vibrant when I left my body, like a reflection on rippling water, but now I felt drab and tragic.

"Westlake wouldn't want to live like this," Mom said. Her jaw stiffened and she nodded. "I know that with absolute certainly. I have always known that."

Mom was right, of course. A future imprisoned in a vegetative state is no future at all, but she'd given up all hope—*belief*—that I would recover. *He's a fighter,* she had said to Dr. Thinker when he'd shown her and Dad the scans of the rotten apple. She didn't think that any more. Neither did Dad. As far as they were concerned, the fight was over.

Mom reached back and clasped Yvette's hand on her shoulder. "You've been so wonderful, Yvette. And I just want you to know that we were still undecided about this when we hired you. We'd talked about it with Georgina, and she . . . well, I guess she didn't want to be around to see how it played out. So she handed in her notice, which was neither helpful nor professional. But you came along, and we've gotten to know you, and that has been a real blessing."

Yvette's pursed lips twitched. Perhaps a smile, or perhaps the realization that she was soon going to be superfluous to requirements.

"How long will you need me for?" she asked.

"Until the end," Mom said, turning to look at her. "I'd understand if you found another caring job and needed to leave, but this is going to be a difficult time for us, and we'd really appreciate your support."

"Yes," Yvette said. She looked at the sun-puddle again. "And when will the tube be disconnected?"

Mom took a deep breath and blinked her wet eyes. "Soon." Barely a word. She clutched Yvette's hand. Dabbed with the Kleenex. "We've met with the doctor. He agrees that it's the best course of action. So now we just need to . . . mentally prepare."

"I understand."

"Do *you* think it's the right course of action, Yvette?" Mom looked at her again. Too many tears to read her expression. Was she hoping Yvette would concur, like Harvey Dent, or disapprove?

I willed her, once again, to say what was on her mind.

To save me.

"It's not my decision," she replied.

"But you can advise," Mom pushed. "That's part of your job description."

"I haven't been working with Westlake long enough to form a professional opinion," Yvette said firmly. "Anything I offer would be unfair, based on intuition rather than medical fact. This matter is between the family and the physician."

Mom nodded and lowered her head.

Every bleak emotion you can think of crowded in on me. My essence—my life force—should have burned them, but they were like kryptonite, and they bested me. My soul *dimmed*. A terrifying feeling. I had always been golden. A vapour. But at that moment, I felt so leaden I was sure Mom and Yvette would hear me clanking through the room. A breeze made of chains. More than anything, I felt betrayed. Too hurt to see any love in their actions. I drooped toward my body, but paused when Mom asked:

"Will you do it, Yvette? Will you remove the tube?"

She'd say no, I was sure of it. Leave it to Harvey Dent. This matter was between the family and the physician, after all. Besides, the whole cracked window thing may have been intuition, but our connection was not. She'd touched my trophies. I'd inhaled the fragrance of her hair, and thought—for a moment that seemed heavenly now, and painfully distant—that she was going to kiss me. Then there was all the time I'd spent with her, wrapped close and healing, wanting to protect her from Wayne. Sure, our connection was intangible, illogical, but it was *real*. No way she'd disconnect my feeding tube. That'd be like pulling the trigger on a gun with excruciatingly slow action.

No way.

I paused. Heavy. Grey.

"Yes," Yvette said. "I can do it."

WESTLAKE SOUL

Is everything a lie? Is any of this really happening? When the things you know and trust break down, when they crumble to dust, reality itself becomes vague. Think of it this way: if you were to look out the window now and see a griffin land in your garden, you wouldn't just question the existence of the griffin . . . you'd question *all* things. Including yourself.

Are you out there? Are you real?

Will you wake up when you die?

Something so ponderous and weighty should cast a shadow, but the sun passed clean through me as I crawled across the garden toward Hub. It occurred to me then— and it has haunted me since—how stupid I had been not to recognize the signs . . . how *blind*. My mind caught fire. Buildings burned and toppled with train-wreck sounds. Smoke jumped up in coral shapes. All of this fuelled by Dr. Quietus's voice: *It's the end of the world, Westlake.* The taste of ashes and loss. My lungs blackened by the truth: *It's all too easy. All the hard work is being done for me. Can't you see that?*

I threw myself next to Hub but he didn't feel me and kept on whining. Nothing I could do to comfort him. Nothing I could say. Too many broken pieces. I waited for the smoke to clear—and it did, eventually, although it revealed nothing but ruin. But I could breathe again. It was a start. And then *think* again . . . if I've ever been able to think at all.

I could contemplate my pain. My despondency.

I had never doubted my parents' faith. I'd assumed it was eternal. And I had never doubted my ability to reward that faith by breaking out of my prison. Beginning with a single, intelligible word. Or smiling on command. Or feeling Mom's hand in mine and squeezing her fingers. Small, yet momentous, steps on the road to recovery. It's all different now, though. The only thing I'm certain of is that Dr. Quietus is bigger and badder than ever. He's closer, too. When Yvette removes my feeding tube, my life expectancy will be down to days. Maybe a couple of weeks, if I'm lucky.

Or *unlucky*, depending on how you look at it.

Either way, doesn't give me much time to "contemplate" a way out.

I need to get smart, baby.

Clock is ticking.

15. Long Fall.

Today is Tuesday, September 20, 2011. It has been a hot summer, but the nights are getting cooler and the leaves are beginning to turn—the merest threads of gold and red, caught only in a certain light. I may see them turn fully, but I doubt I'll see them fall. And I certainly won't see them bud and bloom anew.

My parents have finished their mental preparation. They are ready.

Yvette will remove my tube on Thursday.

I've flown all over the world for surfing tournaments. I didn't mind flying, although I always experienced a jolt of anxiety. I'd look at the fuselage as I boarded the plane and imagine a fragment of it—painted with the airline's colours—smouldering in a field somewhere, surrounded by blistered seats, oddments of luggage, and something that looks like the partial ribcage of a blue whale. I'd see it in my mind with the CNN Breaking News ticker scrolling along the bottom, or as the front page of *The New York Times*, adorned with some tragic headline. (All of this from a glimpse of the fuselage as I boarded, and that's what comes of having a vivid imagination.) It wasn't this fabricated news scene, or the thought of the crash itself—of dying—that unsettled me . . . but rather the thought of the time it would take for the plane to slam down to earth. Three minutes—or however long—of knowing you are about to die, of hearing the screams of the people around you, complete strangers, who know the same. A different timbre of scream. Harrowing. Pushed out on final breaths.

That's what unsettled me.

The *time*.

And that's what I'm experiencing now. My plane has lost all four engines and I'm nosediving toward my doom. I used to think that three minutes was a terrifyingly long time to know that you're about to die, but it's *nothing*—positively heaven—compared to one whole week. Or two.

Screaming all the way.

I won't give up, though. It'll get harder as I get weaker, but I flat-out fucking *refuse* to give up. Same as always . . . Dr. Quietus is going to have a fight on his hands.

For now, though, I need to release. Not to the ocean, or anywhere loud and full of power, but somewhere serene and distant. The moon, perhaps, where I can float above the maria with tears in my eyes, and prepare myself for the long fall.

Maybe I'll stay there. Never come down.

Look up. Can you see me?

I am the man in the moon. Pale and alone.

II
FALLIN'

16. RESOLVE.

Somebody somewhere is writing this down. This I know; I'm a living (at the moment), breathing (again, at the moment) genius. I am relaying information through his or her creative window. A frailty in the wall. So let's dispel any doubts about my superhero abilities. This shiznit is really happening. You may or may not believe me, and that's fine. But somewhere not very far away from you, somebody exists in a vegetative state; in a coma; in locked-in syndrome. By the time you have finished reading this paragraph, ventilators will have been switched off; feeding tubes disconnected; lives shut down.

This is really happening.

Right now.

So consider me (if it's easier) a voice on the wind. A thousand voices. An orchestra. And next time you see a severely disabled person—in a wheelchair, a hospital bed, even on TV—maybe it'll be my voice you hear. I represent the Great Unspoken, the Silent Undead. You'd better believe that makes me a superhero.

Yvette arrives at 10:30 AM tomorrow to remove my

feeding tube. Eighteen hours and six minutes until my life support is discontinued. Although, in a way, it already has been; I had only two feedings yesterday, only one so far today. It's like my parents have mentally disconnected the tube. Maybe they don't see the point in feeding me. Or are gradually adjusting to the concept of not having to. I can understand that, I guess. Just wish my empty stomach would stop cramping. The pain is something I'll have to get used to, and it will only get worse. But to suffer it before my tube is removed seems an unnecessary cruelty. Like having your thumbs screwed prior to being strapped into the electric chair.

I haven't released since returning from the moon. As tempting as it has been to escape, I have concentrated as much time and energy as possible on healing—scars both physical and mental. The Many Worlds Interpretation is a bust. I am a whole human being, flesh and bone, with a twenty-three-year history. Finding a relative branch point is one thing, but accessing it on a quantum level is quite another. I would have greater success with the Many *Minds* Interpretation, a theory that suggests a perpetuity of worlds within one psyche. Though potentially accessible, it is sadly impractical—fuelled as it is by a singular physicality (me, in other words). And when I die, all worlds collapse.

Besides, it's just another form of escape . . . delusion.

Ultimately, the only way out is to repair my body. My cracked window. This won't be any easier than finding a doorway to an alternate reality, but it's real, at least—not based on theory. It's all I've got.

I'm no stranger to the desolate streets of the motor

cortex. I have walked them many times, calling out for help, trying to force my way into buildings with locked doors and boarded-over windows. It's like being a character in a science fiction novel. The Last Man on Earth. A plague has wiped out the rest of mankind, and now—forlorn, shocked, smeared with grime and wearing a torn shirt—I must rebuild. Reading those novels, there's always another survivor that the protagonist eventually encounters, and has to decide whether or not to trust. Or there's a military-run safe haven several hundred miles in the wrong direction that he or she found out about via a fuzzy radio transmission. A vestige of hope. I would give anything for that right now, but the motor cortex truly is deserted. I have gone from aimless wandering to exploring—ransacking. How many doors do I have to knock down to blink? How high do I have to climb to smile? I have pitched my shovel into this barren earth and turned over nothing but soil and flint. How deep are the flexed muscles, the raised eyebrows? When the blade strikes wood, will I have discovered a chest brimming with treasure? (Just imagine: to brush my own hair; to dress myself; to *walk*.) Or will it be the lid of my coffin?

Today I spent six hours trying to twitch my ring finger. On the outside I didn't even break a sweat. Inside I screamed, standing naked in the motor cortex, praying for a breeze to stir the dead leaves, or a few drops of rain to moisten the ground. You want to know what that's like? Okay, do this: place your hand flat on a table with your middle finger curled into your palm. Now move your thumb. Easy, huh? Now move your index finger. No problem. Your pinky. Again, easy. Now move your ring finger . . .

Not so simple, right?

Do that for six hours with stomach cramps crippling your lower body, and the knowledge that if you *don't* move your ring finger, you're going to die.

Yeah. That's what it's like.

All four engines in flames, but I'm not giving up. And I'm focused now. Absolutely. Death is a powerful motivator. It's not like I didn't *try* to find a way out before. I did—often, and earnestly. But I always had time on my side, and was distracted too easily. I'd start chatting to Hub or release somewhere bright, go play with infant gorillas, read over Cormac McCarthy's shoulder. This "deadline" has changed the game. The incentive I needed. If I can't recover now, perhaps I never would have.

Westlake wouldn't want to live like this, Mom had said, and she was right on the money. Moms know best, after all. Tell me I'm going to be like this forever, and I'll tell you to put a fucking bullet in my head. Faith has kept me going, and now it's—literally—do or die time.

I've made my peace with that.

My jaunt to the moon was valuable. A silent and vast plain where I did nothing but *think*. I gained perspective. Bitterness and despondency slipped away, replaced by a cool cube of resolve. I assessed my situation from my parents' point of view and asked the question, *What would I do?* Disturbingly, I didn't have to think about it for long. To imagine a loved one in such an enfeebled state was profoundly upsetting. Would what I do? I'd flick the switch, too. No doubt about it.

Thus, I have decided not to even *try* to divert their course of action. I'd considered swimming through the soup of their thoughts, hoping to breach the protection of their conscious minds, if only to buy myself some time. I could fly a banner through their dreams and hope they would remember it on waking, and that they wouldn't dismiss it as some residue of guilt. But the deadline has become precious. Ominous and terrible, yes . . . but *needed*. It may be the only thing that gets me out of this prison. A scythe-shaped key.

17. WE ARE FAMILY.

Nine hours, thirty-one minutes.

Everything is silent. After all the tears, the house is finally sleeping. I'm wide awake, though, and filled with glassy pain. I hope it abates; the motor cortex is waiting and the clock goes tick-tock. I need to get to work.

But first (and briefly), reflection . . .

Tonight was difficult, but beautiful. So much love for Westlake Soul, but eerily like attending my own funeral. I was fed (probably for the final time) by Mom. She worked quickly, and with noted distraction. *It's okay, Mom*, I said to her. *Don't be sad. I understand.* Her hands trembled. She spilled formula on my sheets. Mopped it away with the towel, leaving a small stain. She poured the rest into the syringe, her brow furrowed. The tan liquid flowed into my stomach and I thought about prisoners on death row, how they get whatever they want for their last meal. Steak, lobster, prime rib—although most choose junk food, and who can blame them for that? I had wondered if Mom would liquefy a couple of rump steaks, French fries, maybe throw in a few onion rings. Pour *that* into my stomach and flush with an ice-cold Budweiser. Didn't happen, though. No death row treatment for this kid. Only thing on the menu was Jevity 1.2 Cal. The same as always. Still, I wouldn't have tasted the liquefied steaks, anyway. No big loss.

The difficult, beautiful moment came an hour or so after my feeding. Dad came in and lifted me into my chair. I groaned and dribbled. He wiped my chin, stroked my face, folded a warm blanket over my legs. Mom and Niki were in the living room, sitting quietly. The TV was off. Kind of rare for this time on a Wednesday (or any) evening. They were missing *Jeopardy*. I deduced things were about to get serious.

My head flopped, hit the buffers and stopped. I groaned again.

"This is going to be a night with Westlake," Dad said, parking my chair in the middle of the room before taking a seat next to Mom. They clasped each other's hands and that was nice to see. "A night *for* Westlake. We don't know how long we're going to have—" And here he stopped and his face stiffened and Mom rubbed his back. "We don't know how long Westlake has got, so we're doing this tonight, as a family, united in our love for him, and with a wish that our beautiful son and brother finds everything he wants in the next life."

Everybody was crying now—*already*, and things were only just getting started. Have to admit, I was crying, too. Impossible not to. I edged from my body to absorb their love, and *felt* it. A real and solid thing that I cradled. The tears in my eyes were too small to see, but they were there. And they were real, too.

Hub came in. Head low. Tail low. He saw everybody

crying, then turned around and walked out. Hub hasn't taken this well—hasn't really been able to face me. He sleeps alone most nights, and gone are the days when he'll jump onto my bed and rest his head on my legs.

I heard his paws clicking down the hallway. The sigh of his body as he sagged onto the floor at the foot of the stairs.

"So here's what we're going to do," Dad continued, wiping his wet cheeks. "It won't be easy, I know, but we're going to watch a few home movies, then we're going to share our favourite memories of Westlake while listening to some of his favourite songs. This is our tribute to him, and our way of showing how deeply he touched—" Dad's words choked to a stop. His face stiffened again and he sobbed, hiding behind one forearm. A full forty seconds before he was able to speak again. "This is already harder than I thought it would be. Anyway, yes . . . our tribute to Westlake, to thank him for bringing us so much joy." Now Dad looked at me. His throat worked as he tried to suppress the sobs. I wanted to fly out of my chair and hold him so tight. "We'll never forget you, buddy," he said. "You'll always be a part of our family . . . our lives."

Mom taught Niki how to fold her Kleenex while Dad selected a few home movies and pushed the first of them into the player. Within moments I was on TV. Baby Westlake. The date in the bottom right corner of the screen read, 04/03/88. Newborn. In Mom's arms, my tiny head snuggled in the pillow of her elbow. Mom was teasing her pinky into my hand and I gripped it tight, my pudgy fingers dimpled, fingernails the size, and shape, of sesame seeds. Cut to Dad holding me, in his hippie days, with hair down to his shoulders and beads in his beard. He was crying on TV, too, but with joy this time. His amazing eyes shone. His hair then was the same colour as mine now. My scrunched little face pressed against his chest, content in the fierce glow of his sun.

We watched home movies for an hour and a half—a window on a world where only happiness existed. My first Christmas. First birthday. Three years old, my face covered with vanilla ice cream (you can hear Mom and Dad laughing their asses off in the background). Aged six, holding Niki for the first time (her tiny hand curled around my pinky). Three different Halloweens, dressed as a zombie, a vampire, an Oreo Cookie. Two vacations, one in Disney World (screaming at Goofy—the seven-foot-tall version, which still looks freaky, even today), the other camping in Algonquin Park (Dad pretending to be a bear, chasing his squealing, delighted children around a tree). Eight years old, playing soccer, my hair almost white in the sun. A little older, on a swing set behind Aunt Janey's house. I kick my legs and soar, wanting to loop-the-loop— unafraid, even then. Me and Mom playing Twister, and I'm laughing because her ass is in my face. Fourteen years old, my first surfboard, Dad filming me as I tackle ankle busters at Cocoa Beach. Sixteen years old, play-wrestling Niki, giving her a noogie.

This and more. A boat of memories sailing only tranquil waters. Just a regular kid, a regular family. And it reminded me how much I used to smile. We *all* did. The frickin' happy family—like we lived on Sesame Street, or something. Only my life, or my death (eventually), will bring those smiles back. This in-between state is destructive in so many ways. I welcome the end of it. One way or another.

So we watched home movies as darkness edged all red light from the sky. Niki moved to the sofa and sat with Mom and Dad and they hugged each other and wept, and sometimes they laughed or commented on this and that, but mostly they wept. Strange tears. Melancholic, yet touched with joy. I wondered if they were differently shaped. I took their love and pressed against it. Nobody saw my upper lip twitch. Almost a smile. Nobody saw the tear curve around my cheekbone, fall from my jaw.

Dad had burned a CD of some of my favourite tunes. He'd done a pretty good job, too. A good selection of upbeat (AC/DC, The White Stripes, Kings of Leon) and suitably depressing (Coldplay, Radiohead, Leonard Cohen), along with a few classics from the likes of The Beatles and Hendrix. He turned off the TV and put this on, and for the next hour or so they shared their favourite Westlake memories. Again, a good selection, and I listened through alternating waves of pride, sadness, and joy. At one point, Niki got up from the sofa, crouched beside my chair, and held my hand. She squeezed my fingers, like she was a baby again. She shared her memories with a smile and I can't recall a time that I was more proud of her. It crushed me that I couldn't thank her for being my sister, and my friend. Mom and Dad danced to Cohen's "Famous Blue Raincoat." Dad had his arms crossed over Mom's back, pulling her close. Mom's head was on his chest, eyes closed and wet. Every now and then Dad would kiss the top of her head. They shared everything. Pain was huge and real, but in that moment, as Cohen sang, it was manageable, small enough to hold.

"More," Mom said, and grinned.

"Another dance?" Dad asked.

"Maybe later," Mom said. "More."

Dad frowned. Niki, too.

"*Mooooore*," Mom said again. "Don't you remember? That was how Westlake used to say Mom. It was his first word."

Dad nodded and kissed her. "Always Mommy's little boy."

"He adored his Daddy, too."

"*Gaaaah*," Dad said. "That's how he said it—like he had something stuck in his throat."

I smiled inside, brought the memory forward: Gaah and More, their large faces hovering over me. The sun and the moon. Dad would always laugh because, when I was hungry, I'd point at Mom's breast and say, "More . . . *Mooooore*." So much time had passed. The world had shifted. I'd gone from being a regular kid with an infinite smile to a broken thing. A shell. But they were still Gaah and More—the sun and the moon—to me.

The music stopped and there was silence. It stretched, almost to the point where it ached, and I knew what they were thinking without having to dip into their minds: *Are we doing the right thing?* This was not something they were seriously considering, and certainly nobody said it out loud. I wished I could put their minds at ease—assure them that I understood their decision, sympathized with their situation. My head flopped to the other side. Mom and Dad nodded. A small but resolute gesture. Niki broke the silence by blowing her nose.

They kissed me goodnight. Niki first. High on the cheekbone. She squeezed my hand again. "I love you," she said. Then Mom, her fingers in my hair, her kiss on the side of my mouth, and the muscles in my lips tried to react, reciprocate. "Sweet dreams, baby," she said. Dad wheeled me through to the groovy room and lifted me into bed. He pulled the sheets up, tucked me in, then cupped my face in one hand. "You're the son I always wanted, and the son I'll always have. I'm so proud of you." His kiss landed square in the middle of my forehead. He left my room, in tears again.

Gaah, I thought.

They talked for a little longer and I left them to it. I wanted to work but was too emotional. So I lay there and stared at the ceiling. Mostly gloom, but the door was half open so I could see a wedge of Surf City Blue in the light from the hallway. Niki eventually went to bed. I heard her computer ping and click as she checked her e-mail and updated her Facebook status. Then the bed springs bounced and she flicked off the light. Soon afterward, very softly, "Famous Blue Raincoat" again. Mom and Dad dancing, holding each other close.

A beautiful, difficult evening. A celebration of a life I haven't quite finished living. Everybody is sleeping now, including Hub. He moved into the living room when Mom and Dad went to bed—walked past my door without looking in.

Silence.

Almost.

I can hear him. Dr. Quietus. Close by. He won't come for me tonight; he just wants me to know he's there. His laughter is the sound of breaking bones. His breathing is the wind in a narrow space. If I could walk to the window and pull open the blinds, I would see him. Floating in the dark. Hands pressed to the glass. Eyes like clock faces, watching me.

18. Virtual Reality.

I worked through the night—lit a fire in the motor cortex to see if I could excite some movement. The heat was incredible but I had no choice but to endure it. Sweating, coated in ashes, I tried to move my left thumb, then my left foot. Hours passed like grave soldiers marching rhythmically to battle, knowing they may never return. I thought—and how my heart leapt!—that I had succeeded when my left leg jerked beneath the sheets. Pain gripped my pelvis, drove screws to the bone. The movement was involuntary, though; I fanned the flames and tried again, but there was nothing.

I succumbed to exhaustion at some deep time and slept motionless while the clock carried on ticking, as if my bed and I had been sculpted from the same slab of granite. My dreams were unkind. Parents with scissors. Headless babies. I was too tired to control them. I awoke to the light of midmorning and a truckload of pain. In my legs. My stomach. My shoulders. I stared at the walls. A muscle in my forearm twitched. It was 9:42 AM.

Forty-eight minutes.

Already so weak, already failing, and my tube hadn't even been removed. I needed to recharge and get my emotions in check—ready myself for battle. I was tempted to release. To the moon again, or to some cold, clear mountain where I could roost with eagles and fly above the world in a startling M-shape. I was afraid, though, that if I released I would never come back. How easy, to admit defeat and reside in bliss until the end. But not an option. And so I did the next best thing. I daydreamed.

Blissfully.

Virtual reality: a computer-generated environment that uses software and hardware to deceive the user's senses. But here's the deal: reality *can* be a state of mind. To believe that what we are experiencing is real . . . to see, touch, and smell . . . to feel emotion. We experience this every night when we go to sleep and surrender to the subconscious. *Dreaming* is virtual reality. No computer required.

I can control this reality. Another benefit of having flipped the iceberg, although one I rarely take advantage of. Dreams are like waves; they're not always easy, but you just have to ride them. Daydreams are a little different— pedestals for fantasies. Here you can flex the muscle of your imagination, and indeed you *should*. Because of my familiarity with the id, I can achieve total absorption in my daydreams. I can touch, hear, taste . . . *experience*. Virtual reality, baby. And because my dreams had been so cruel, I decided to treat myself, to take a moment and recuperate here . . .

Deep *in a fairy tale forest. Golden pine needles underfoot and a thousand different trees* trembling like cold men. "Where are you taking me, baby?" Yvette asks. I brush the hair from one side of her face and see that her eyes are blue, but then she steps toward me, into a subtly different light, and they shift to green. I blink, my lips pulled into half a smile. "How do you do that?" I ask, and Yvette shrugs. "That thing with your eyes?" She kisses me and steps back and does it again. Green to blue. I imagine her irises like kaleidoscope glass. "Where are you taking me?" she asks again. I tell her it's a surprise, take her hand, and lead her through the woods. Through pillars of sunlight and sprays of wild grass. Petals and burrs cling to our clothes. Nature is the sound of breathing. We are barefoot. I look down and see tiny sequins embedded in the polish on her toenails. They flicker, blue and green, and I have to concentrate to keep my feet on the ground. Maybe Yvette senses this because she clutches my hand tighter, like a child clutching a balloon string. We carry on walking, scooping fragrant air into our lungs. Yvette occasionally remarks on the birds and flowers, all of burning colour, or copper-coated fawns standing in bars of light. "I feel like I'm in a Disney cartoon," she says. We are walking so close together that her shoulder bumps my arm. I am taller than her. My muscles are firm and real. "We're nearly there," I say, and a moment later we hear the music. "A piano?" Yvette asks. "In the forest?" And I tell her that anything is possible. We walk a little *faster, toward the music, and step at last into a clearing bordered by amazing trees. Sunlight strikes the raised lid of a grand piano (an 1896 Steinway Model B, just like Nadia's, but I don't tell Yvette this) that is being played by Alicia Keys. A melody to fit the mood. Delicate and dreamlike. Yvette gasps, covers her mouth with one hand, and looks at me in disbelief. I smile and point to the centre of the clearing, where a table for two has been set. Two roses in a crystal vase, champagne on ice, glimmering silverware. Johnny Depp is our waiter. He wears a white tuxedo and his hair is long and messy, like it was in* What's Eating Gilbert Grape? *"What's going on here?" Yvette asks, and I reply, "I just want everything to be perfect." We eat exotic foods until our mouths are sweet and stained, and then dance around the clearing as Alicia plays. Moonlight replaces sunlight. Shades of silver and white. Johnny's suit glows. Then we break from the clearing and run like wood nymphs through the trees, discarding our clothes. We are naked when we arrive at the waterfall. It is so high, and so stained by light, that it appears to fall from the moon and into a pool that could be filled with mercury. Yvette dives in first. A perfect silhouette in the air. Barely a splash as she meets the cold water. I follow with equal grace, swim deep, my lungs filled with silver oxygen. I find Yvette and we shimmer, then break the surface together. The moon pours onto us. Through the trees, amid the high sound of falling water and night birds, we can still hear Alicia play. "Why did you bring me here?" Yvette asks. We are so close, I can feel her hair on my shoulder. "Because you're good for me," I reply. "And I need to heal . . . to get strong for what lies ahead." She frowns and I kiss her before she can say anything else. We sink into the water and I imagine her closing those blue/green eyes, and in that moment I know that dreams are the reality that sustain life.*

And I *needed* this. I don't care if it's sentimental bullshit. I needed—more than ever before, and if only for a heartbeat—to exist in a world where everything was perfect, and where Yvette loved me. Imagine the cracked window repaired. Better yet, imagine it replaced with stained glass. A sheet of light and colour. You don't just see through this window, you *experience* it. I could feel the pine needles beneath my feet. Smell the wild forest. Hear Alicia play. Taste the food that Johnny served. Yvette in my arms—*in my arms*. Holding her, kissing her. The moon pouring onto us. Her eyes changed from blue to green, then back again.

Virtual reality. Just like dreaming.

Healing.

I snapped, regretfully, out of it, but stronger, into a reality that I would never—*could* never—invent. My broken body propped against pillows. My wall of achievement, gathering dust. The sound of Yvette's Beetle pulling into the driveway.

10:28 AM.

19. Westlake: Unplugged.

Dr. Harvey Dent (or Dr. Two-Face, if you prefer, and I think that seems more fitting) told my parents that I wouldn't feel any pain while I slowly starved to death. He said I'd simply, and peacefully, fade away. No doubt this made Mom and Dad's decision a mite easier. Anything that is easier is good for them, I suppose, and they'll never know any different; I can't contradict Dr. Two-Face by communicating the incredible pain I'm already feeling. My parents will witness my deterioration—they'll listen to my scratchy breaths and wipe the blood from my lips—but all the time they'll be unaware that I'm screaming inside.

Dr. Two-Face is wrong. It hurts. So much. Already.

I thought Yvette's hair would still be wet from the pool, or that I'd smell the forest on her skin. It took a few moments to adjust to seeing her dressed in plain work clothes with her hair tied back. She looked in on me briefly before having coffee with my parents (Dad had taken the morning off work), where there was little of the small talk one might normally enjoy over a mug of joe. It was quickly to business. Dad and Mom confirmed the decision to remove my PEG tube, and Yvette told them what to expect in the coming days/weeks. I will become drawn and pale. Will lose body mass rapidly. My skin will dry and flake away. My hair could thin and fall out. There will be bleeding from my eyes and mouth as my mucous membranes dry up and crack. My breathing, toward the end, will be rapid and grating.

"It's going to be difficult," Yvette said. "Upsetting."

"Dr. Kellerman told us that Westlake wouldn't feel any pain." Mom looked into her coffee. "He said it would be peaceful."

"I'm a trained healthcare professional, not a doctor," Yvette said. "I can't comment on Westlake's condition, or whether or not he feels pain. It may well be peaceful for him, but it certainly won't be for you."

"We understand," Dad said.

"And you know that his feeding tube can be reinserted," Yvette said, "if you have a change of heart?"

"Yes," Dad said.

Mom nodded.

I'd spent some time thinking about my PEG tube, and how its removal was a symbolic gesture—an underscoring of my parents' decision more than a discontinuance of life support. They didn't *need* to remove it, after all; they could have left it dangling from my stomach and simply discontinued my feeds. But there's a psychological edge to not having anything through which to feed me (even though, as Yvette said, the tube could be reinserted at any point). Removing it cemented their decision. But more, it stated that they didn't believe I would recover. The equivalent of a trainer throwing in his boxer's towel.

I'm still fighting, though, despite it being hard. Probably impossible. And yet, no harder than seeing my parents lose hope. I admit to a moment's panic—assailing their minds in an effort to divert their course of action. Forget empathy and understanding. Disregard what I said about needing a deadline. I leapt first into Dad's mind and directed my flashlight through a fog of ones and zeroes. *Dad, it's me, Westlake . . . don't do this. Please don't give up on me. . . .* I heard my words echoing off his wall. That insurmountable barricade of reason. He frowned, as if he were trying to remember something, and swirled the dregs of his coffee. Nothing more. I recalled the time they'd forgotten about me—left me on the rear deck as night fell. I'd rapped on Dad's mind then and gotten a similarly vague response. It was the same now; I was left outside and night was falling. I flowed then into Mom's mind, screaming her name, knowing she wouldn't hear me. Ever get the feeling someone is watching you? That's what Mom felt. She looked up from her coffee, glanced over her shoulder.

"What is it?" Dad asked.

"Nothing," she said.

I slipped from their locked-down minds and returned to my mountain. A sheer, demanding climb.

"Okay," Yvette said.

Mom and Dad stayed in the kitchen, silent, clasping hands, while Yvette removed my tube. It only took thirty seconds. There was no melancholy soundtrack. No angry mob protesting outside, waving placards with LET WESTLAKE LIVE emblazoned on them. It was all rather unspectacular. Yvette merely snapped on her gloves and pulled the tube from my stomach (excruciating pain as the bumper securing the tube from inside passed through the stoma, but I didn't even flinch). There was a spurt of blood and gastric fluid that Yvette quickly wiped away. She then covered the open hole with gauze and surgical tape, and that was it. Job done. She disposed of the detritus, and I looked at her as the pain (all too slowly) faded. It struck me as cruel that she should be so beautiful—that she had gone from starring in my virtual reality, a source of strength and inspiration, to being the one who had finalized my parents' loss of hope. It would have been easier if she'd looked like a wicked stepmother.

Okay, that's not fair. My parents—following numerous consultations with specialists—had requested Yvette perform a duty as a healthcare professional, and she had done so. Nothing wicked about that. But I couldn't get over her detachment. This was the same woman who had touched my trophies, rubbed calamine lotion into my burned skin, and trailed her finger through the strip of hair beneath my bellybutton. Always with such compassion. *Everybody thinks he is broken, but he is still intact*, she had said to her mother. Yet she had discontinued my life support with cold efficiency. She hadn't even looked me in the eye.

I know that such detachment is necessary, but I wonder how much of the pain I felt when she removed my PEG tube was emotional. It had burned, and hurt more than I thought it would. Also, despite my gift for perfect recollection, Yvette is drawn differently when I think about those thirty seconds now. Her softness is blurred. Her eyes are blank, neither blue nor green. This is my doing, of course. My emotion. I appear determined to soften my disappointment by recreating her as Atropos. A woman of grim duty who, with her abhorred shears, severs the thread of life.

And really, what was I expecting? That melancholy soundtrack? Her tears falling on my chest, warm and fat, like summer rain?

I should learn to keep fantasies in my mind.

Either way, it is done. No more tube. No more nutrition or hydration.

"Let's hope it's quick," Dad said.

I'm on my own.

I have spent the last thirty-one hours fighting my condition. A relentless battle that brought no gain. Time to sleep, and hopefully rest. Find a dream with no fight, no pain, and no Dr. Quietus. Tomorrow I'll do it all over again.

Before I sleep, though, I'm just going to hang a while. Endure the pain. Niki is sitting in the Mork chair, doing something out of character. She's singing. Loud and unabashed. Bob Dylan's "I Shall Be Released." So apt I could cry. At least it's not "Knocking on Heaven's Door."

I listen. Unresponsive. My throat dry and sore.

Her voice carries me. Like the sweetest arms.

She finishes. Sits silently.

I think I should close my eyes. And I do.

20. THE FUCKTARD STRIKES AGAIN.

I haven't forgotten about Wayne. I'm still going to get that son of a bitch.

Four days since my life support was cut off. I have spent most of that time fighting. I have rebuilt the Soulmobile, and drive regularly through the motor cortex, leaping chasms like frickin' Knight Rider, crashing into weakened buildings that separate in spinning pieces. Pedal to the metal. Nothing but speed. I have discovered new terrain but it is just as barren as everywhere else. I drive until the tires are smoking. The headlights uncover a lifelessness that could be measured in light years. One time I popped the hood and ran jumper cables from the battery (a billion volts—that sucker is *juiced*) to deep in my brain: the thalamus—a kind of signal box for sensory and motor function. I gunned the ignition. There was a bang and a curl of blue flame. I expected my body to jerk upright in bed, eyes wide and alive. Returning to the groovy room, I found nothing but a breathing corpse with dry blood on its lips.

I find thin relief in my daydreams, and rest in what

sleep I manage to get, which isn't much. It is broken by pain. My muscles ache from *trying* to work. My stomach, which I imagine hissing and bleeding like a collapsed lung, stages violent demonstrations from head to toe, toppling cars and throwing petrol bombs. My throat is so dry I can feel the lining crumble as I breathe.

My family are doing their best. Staying as strong as they can. There are fewer tears now that they have made their decision, but the distress is a storm. They just want it to be over, and who can blame them? Until then they exhibit cracked smiles and operate on 3% of the iceberg. They're aliens in pretty skins. I float with them sometimes, and study their distraction. Dad is trying to carry on as normal, but keeps missing the mark. Little things. Pouring milk instead of cream into his coffee. Backing the car into the garage door. Too many to mention them all. Niki is out most of the time. Or sleeping. When she's home (and awake) she'll often sit in with me. Curled into the Mork chair, like a chick in an egg, reading something for school or—her new thing—singing. It's crazy how much she loves me. I always knew it . . . but I never really *knew* it, you know? Mom is a cardboard cutout with a distant expression, placed randomly around the house. She graduates, occasionally, to animation, and with short-lived gusto. I watched her drop and do three push-ups on the kitchen floor, then fill out an online application to appear on *Mantracker*. She vacuums in bursts. Designed a tattoo.

And then there's Hub.

He's just so sad all the time. Pooches around the house, eyes down. *It's like he knows*, Dad said to Mom over dinner. No appetite. Not a flick of the tail. He's like a different dog—hasn't said more than a dozen words to me since the tube came out.

Not cool, dude, I said to him. *I could really use your support.*

I know, he whined. *But I'm not there yet.*

He's such a tragic little character. The quintessential pining dog.

Yvette comes every day. Other than not feeding me or having to change my man-diapers, her duties are pretty much the same. My condition is monitored and documented, and I usually get a sup of fresh air while my bedsheets are changed. I'm shaved, washed, and dressed in clean clothes—not for comfort, but to keep my deteriorating body from smelling too bad. She talks to me, like she used to, as if nothing has changed. Sometimes she strokes my hair.

She still stars in my daydreams, and I still wish she were mine. Yeah, for all those lovelorn reasons (I may be wilting, but I can still *feel*), but also because the one man who *is* with her—who can share himself and accept the things she shares—does not deserve her.

I'm not the only one in need of a saviour.

She came in with bruises on her arms yesterday.

It's difficult to equate this bruised girl with the detached, assertive woman who removed my life support. Shit, everybody is multifaceted. It's the reason Dr. Phil can't count all his money. I just wish Yvette would rotate the geometry of her character and show Wayne the strength she shows me. If she would, the bruises would stop.

But she can't. Or won't. Which is why I need to step in.

I don't have much time between work and rest, but I give what I can, and have seen Wayne continue his acts of unkindness. Nothing as brutal as punching her in the eye. A cruel word here. A sneer there. One time he flipped the bird behind her back for no reason other than that he's stupid and mean. On another, he wiped a booger on her pillow. So much anger inside him. I know because I *felt* it—a cold and solid block of anger. He either doesn't know how to deal with it, or doesn't know it's there.

I follow Yvette. I lay on her like a blanket and try to absorb her unhappiness, that I may spirit it away to wherever I am going. And, like Wayne's anger, I can feel it. Pebbles of discontent. I gather what I can, but it's not nearly enough. Prevention being better than the cure, I follow Wayne, too. In glimpses. All I can stand. I ride shotgun in that APPETITE FOR CONSTRUCTION pickup and study the man behind the wheel. His aura thumps as darkly as the music from the stereo. The muscle in his jaw jumps as he grits his teeth. Over and over.

Wayne lives in a two-bedroom apartment in Mathias. I thought it'd be a rundown shithole, but it's actually clean and modern. Real hardwood flooring (son of a bitch always kicks his boots off at the door), a sixty-inch 3D TV, a closet full of cool threads. I guess he's not *always* a thug. Doesn't mean he's not always a fucktard. He just knows when to keep it hidden. Like when he's working. I have to admit, he knows how to run a business—works hard and has a knack for keeping his customers happy. When not banging his hammer or spending time with Yvette, Wayne pumps weights, plays hockey, and hangs with his buddies. He watches UFC and goes to strip clubs. Just an all-Canadian guy, but with a thick strip of meanness.

I can't watch him with Yvette all the time, but with

every slight I have heard, every upturned lip I have seen, I feel my emotion swell. It's exhausting, but I fight. I gauge his biofield and draw from it, computing the minutia, recreating it inside me.

I didn't see him bruise Yvette's arm. Didn't see her ease the swelling on her shoulder with a packet of frozen peas wrapped in a hand towel. I was there, though, when he called her a dumb French whore and made her cry. I was there when he slapped her ass—playful, perhaps, but hard. *Way* too hard. He grinned and flowed through me, and I collected the bricks of his anger, stacked them inside.

She can go from happy to heartbroken in next to no time. This is Wayne's superpower.

Like me, you're probably asking how Yvette could ever have been attracted to someone like Wayne. Everybody makes mistakes, I guess, and she met him when she was vulnerable, and alone, having recently moved away from her family. She recognized early on that Wayne was damaged, and dangerous, but ever the caregiver, she thought she could fix him. And there were moments, particularly at the beginning, when he shone in her eyes. When he showered, shaved, and dressed in his cool threads, he was handsome enough to have stepped from an Abercrombie and Fitch ad. He'd walk into a bar holding her hand, and she felt protected, and he was so strong that he could scoop her into one arm, and all the vulnerability of being away from her family was swept away. Even when things weren't good, which was often the case, she saw hope in Wayne. She felt she could connect with him in a way that nobody had before—that she could pluck the diamond from the rough, and they would both shine.

She couldn't reach him, though. That's what it came down to. Couldn't *help* him. Sometimes people think they have a bond—something special and enduring—when all they have is a trail of broken pieces.

Like I said . . . everybody makes mistakes.

I reached Yvette, however. I *know* I did, despite the cool efficiency with which she removed my feeding tube. I *inspired* her. Quite an achievement from the midst of my vegetative state. (Imagine what I could do with the full use of my body.) She had admired my Wall of Achievement—recognized that pride is not a sin, after all—and had made her own. She took the two framed diplomas from the back of her closet and hung them in pride of place. Then she put up shelves and lined them with the gymnastics trophies she pulled from a box that had been hidden in the same place. They glimmered in the soft light of her living room. Figurines in postures that depict the grace with which they were won. It was a splendid display, and Yvette would often look at it, always smiling, recalling, perhaps, the occasions she had been awarded those accolades. You can imagine how this made me feel, and at a time of such helplessness. I would look at her wall with pride for us both. Achievements should never be lauded, but always noted. Take it from me, you never know when the ability to achieve—even something so small—will be stripped away.

Wayne didn't see it this way.

"The fuck is this?"

"Some trophies I won. That's my college diploma. That's—"

"Dancing?"

"Gymnastics."

He sneered, tested the shelves for sturdiness, gave his head a little shake. I could sense his meanness boiling just beneath the surface, ready to spill over. Yvette's Wall was a challenge to his alpha role—something he *didn't* have, and which (in his own small mind) demeaned him. Guys like Wayne don't appreciated being demeaned.

"The shelves aren't level."

"I did the best I could."

"Did you at least screw into the studs?"

"Of course."

"You surprise me."

She smiled, as if he were making a joke and not being mean. He sneered again to assure her he was. Hoping to diffuse the sudden spike in tension, Yvette stroked his arm, sat on the sofa, and patted the seat next to her.

"Sit with me, baby," she said. "We'll watch a movie."

But Wayne wasn't interested in watching a movie; he wanted to reestablish his alpha role. I could see what he was going to do and tried to stop him. I threw my useless ghost in the way but his arm passed right through. He grabbed one of the trophies and, with no effort at all, snapped the little figure from the top.

"Plastic," he said. "I thought it was real gold."

The argument that followed was brief but ugly, culminating in Wayne breaking three more trophies and thumping Yvette's college diploma with the side of his fist, hard enough for the glass to shatter in its frame. She cried and dropped to the floor, hands covering her head. Wayne stood over her. One hundred percent alpha. Showing his teeth. His fist bled.

Yvette's Wall of Achievement was in pieces behind him.

His aura glimmered like the trophies he had just destroyed. Not gold, but miserable flashes of black and red. It emanated from inside him. Sick energy. I could hear his teeth grinding. The crazy drum of his heart. I moved in front of the door and waited. The TV chirped in the background, ludicrous commercials that couldn't have been more out of place. Wayne made a sound like he was clearing his throat, told Yvette to go fuck herself, and then left. But he passed through me on his way to the door and I opened my arms wide. I took his anger. A hard and heavy haul. Not one brick but dozens. Enough to build a wall. I added them to the pile—now a towering, teetering stack— and went to Yvette. Ghost hands stroked her hair, her face. I flowed through her, gathering blocks of anguish.

I went home with all of this inside me. I listened to Niki sing, and her voice soothed me. *Healed* me, almost.

My left eye blinked in time with the melody.

Work. Deep in the motor cortex. Screaming into emptiness, losing track of time as my body deteriorates. But no, I haven't forgotten about Wayne the Fucktard. He is one supervillain I *will* get the better of.

Soon . . . I'll get to him soon.

And I think I know how.

21. Rainbows.

Blood oozing from my anus. Not very superhero-like, huh? You never read *that* line in *The Amazing Spider-Man*, did you? My bedsheets had to be changed three times yesterday (I'm back in my diapers today). The tip of my penis is as dry as—and somewhat resembles—dead fruit. Hair falling out. Armpits clogged with flaky skin. Veins I didn't even know I had showing in my face. Stomach a broad dip, like something that could catch water. Hip bones poking up. I breathe like a cat hissing.

Nine days without food.

Everything—*everything*—hurts.

Tomorrow is the first day of October. Always my favourite month, when the colours come to life and the night draws in close and cold. There's a real feeling of change in the air, more so than any other time of the year. Spring in Ontario moves quickly. Nobody can quite believe the snow has stopped, and before we know it the sidewalks are baking and we're drinking beer on the patio. Autumn is different. It's patient; it fades in and out, a considerate season. The colours begin in September, but in October they burn and fall. Kind of like me, all engines blazing. Forgive my lapse into poetic metaphor, but to think of a leaf, once healthy, quickly withering and burning, falling to the ground . . . it's appropriate that October should be the month of my death.

No change in the homestead, though. Apart from a few tender moments spent with me, Mom, Dad, and Niki shuffle around, pale-faced and brainless, like extras in a George Romero flick. The occasional smile or half-hearted attempt at conversation, but that's it. Sometimes I think their life is as distant as mine. Hub hasn't wagged his tail for over two weeks. He spends most of his time with Niki. She scratches his belly. His leg twitches and his tongue lolls, but the dude isn't happy.

It'll get easier, for everybody, once it's over.

A matter of days now. That's all I have. This narrative could—and probably will—simply end, without resolve. Which reflects life in general, I think. We rarely get the opportunity to tie up loose ends and finish neatly. We quite often end mid-sentence.

I woke from dreams like clenched fists to see Dr. Quietus floating above my bed. This was two nights ago. He snapped his teeth and swirled but didn't touch me. I waited to be dragged into what would surely be our final battle—and one he would win—but it never happened. I inhaled his thick stink and shuddered, and he eventually faded, soaking into the dark air like a puddle into the ground.

He's here with me now. He fades, but never leaves.

Any moment, baby.

I look like a scarecrow with all the straw blown from

its shirt. I have sunken eyes and my teeth are too large in my face, projecting from gums you could strike matches off. There may as well be an hourglass poised above my head, the last grains of sand sifting through. Mom and Dad aren't Catholic, or religious in any way, so there'll be no Last Rites. Only their final goodbyes, which they have already made.

Darryl came to say goodbye, too. A brief visit, and hard for him. I wish I could have leapt out of bed and kicked his ass out the door. Not because I didn't appreciate the visit, but to spare him the discomfort. He didn't want to be anywhere near me. Dad called him, told him that I was fading fast and that he should come and say goodbye. Darryl made some bullshit excuse about having to go to Kitchener with his boss. "Forget that," Dad said to him. "Get your ass here and say goodbye to your best friend." And so he did, and he stayed as long as he could bear. Almost seven minutes. He stood by the door, biting his fingernails, glancing at me, then quickly away.

"Dude," he said, over and over.

I jumped into his mind, converted the data. He was thinking about Michael Jackson in the "Thriller" video. The part where he's a zombie, dancing in the street with a horde of equally nimble undead. Then he got to thinking about how he once dressed up as Michael Jackson for Halloween and moonwalked for treats.

"Dude," he said.

So I looked like a zombie to him, one that might—at any time—begin body popping. I groaned and he backed against the wall, perhaps fearing I would spring out of bed and bite his arm. It was all too much for him. He pulled a grim face and looked down at his crisp white socks.

"You're a good guy, Wes," he said. "When I remember you . . . I'll remember the old you. The *real* you. We kicked ass, huh?"

I tried to nod. To wink. Foul breath creaked from my open mouth.

"Here, you can have this," he said, reaching into his jeans pocket and pulling out something I'd coveted for nearly three years: Angus Young's guitar pick—flicked into the crowd at our first AC/DC concert. Darryl had snatched it from the air, quick and accurate, like a frog catching a fly. "I figure it'd be pretty sick to be, you know, buried with it."

Cremated, I said. *But yeah . . . pretty sick.*

He stepped forward, but then stopped and looked at his socks again. A deep breath. Another glance at me.

It's all good, Darryl, I said. *I know I'm hungry, but I promise not to eat your brain.*

"Okay," he said, as if he'd heard me. Three hesitant steps (you'd think a gigantic scorpion's stinger extended from the collar of my pyjamas, hooked to strike), then at full stretch he placed the pick on my nightstand. I wanted to, and *tried* to, reach out and clasp his arm—what a hoot!— but couldn't, of course. He scampered back to the door and puffed out his cheeks like he'd just successfully navigated a minefield.

"Dude," he said. "Be seeing you."

Then he was gone. I heard his synergy green Camaro roar into the distance. He'd left rubber on our driveway.

No other visitors. They may come in the next few days, but I doubt it. Aunt Janey lives in Poughkeepsie, NY, and I haven't seen her since I was eleven years old. She and

Mom don't see eye to eye. Grandma Soul—my one living grandparent—has been detached from reality for a long time. She's not senile, she's just . . . well, *out there*. She lives on an intentional community (read: hippie commune) in Florida, and has made a small fortune selling bottles of ocean air labelled as Good Vibrations (ingredients: peace and love). Dad e-mailed to tell her that I'm not long for this world. Grandma Soul replied with a link to an Ojibwa prayer on YouTube, and an assurance that a motherly hand was poised to carry my spirit to the earth's energy stream. She added that she wouldn't be making the long trip north to say goodbye in person, but would send a rainbow in her stead. And wouldn't you know it, that rainbow appeared. Dad wheeled me onto the rear deck and we watched it fade from the sky together.

"That's a gift from Grandma Soul," Dad assured me.

Just a coincidence, but it was sweet that he believed it.

Goodbye. Such a simple word, and so often delivered without feeling. Almost without thought. An automatic response, like an ATM flashing, *THANK YOU HAVE A NICE DAY!* It's because, when saying goodbye, we invariably assume that we will see that person again. Some time. Some place. But the word has different power when we know that it truly *is* goodbye—when that person is leaving our life forever. A final goodbye is a weight that drags and pulls.

It's not easy. Mom, Dad, and Niki have voiced it in different ways. Knowing that I can go at any time, they have each ventured into the groovy room for some final Wes-time—to say *adios* should they not get another chance.

"I think I want to be a singer," Niki said. "Fuck getting a regular job. That's *so* not for me. And I don't want kids because they just get hurt—at some point they *all* get hurt—and I can't handle that. So I'm totally going to learn the guitar, and I'm going to be a singer. A *real* singer. Like that woman Dad likes. Joni someone."

Mitchell, I said.

"You know . . . sings that song about the parking lot."

Big Yellow Taxi, I said.

She sat in the Mork chair, swinging her legs, twisting her hair. She's seventeen but every time I look at her—I swear to God—she's still a little girl. My kid sister. Breaks my heart, because I want to be her big brother again. Wrap my arms around her. I want to be cool in her eyes, and protect her from the world.

"I don't care about being famous," she continued. "That's not what it's about. I'll write songs with pretty melodies and communicate what I'm feeling inside. All the hurt. The disappointment. I'll play bars and clubs, maybe a few folk festivals. Record an album that doesn't sell. Then I'll totally develop a drinking problem, go to rehab, and probably convert to Buddhism."

She looked out the window, where the leaves burned. She wiped her eyes with her fingers before the tears could fall. Her eyelashes flickered.

"I've got it all planned," she said. "It's going to be awesome."

I prefer to imagine a future with Niki in rhapsody. Not taking the Amy Winehouse route, but being strong and confident, flourishing in her intelligence and beauty. Not childless, either. Niki would make an incredible mother— all that love—and would accept, even *embrace*, that children get hurt. But they heal, too. They *learn*.

Hurt strengthens the wall.

My shallow stomach trembled. The dry skin in the crook of my left arm cracked and seeped.

Niki sang:

For one more chance to hear you laugh,
To see you smile, watch you surf,
Brother, nothing could stop me,
No man. No god.
If I could take your pain, I would.

Better than Angus Young's guitar pick. Better than Grandma Soul's rainbow.

So much love. It towered.

"That's all I've got so far," she said. "I wrote it this morning. It's called 'Brother.' It'll be the first track on the album."

She fell silent. Grey light played on her face and her eyelashes seemed too bright.

I couldn't say anything. Not even inside.

Dad didn't sing, but he still gave me something: a confession. It had been heavy on his heart for a number of years. I suppose he thought telling someone would help ease the load—it usually does—and, perhaps, dilute the sin. A reverse deathbed confession. Who better to share your transgression with than someone who will—very soon—take it to the grave?

"To this day your mother has no idea how close I came to leaving her—leaving you all." He was wearing his tan leatherette waistcoat, which he loved because he said it was like something Dennis Hopper would wear in his prime.

Only, with his sandy hair and beard, it made him look like Dr. Zaius from *Planet of the Apes*. "It was a long time ago. Just after Niki was born. Your mother had a bad case of postpartum depression. Real bad. We also had financial concerns. So I spent more time at work, partly to steer clear of your mother, but mostly to put a bigger number on my paycheque. This meant spending more time with my co-workers. One in particular. Rosemary Fuller."

You dirty son of a bitch, I said.

"Twenty-six years old and beautiful. Jesus, she looked like Cameron Diaz, I'm not kidding. We were involved for about seven months. I fell in love with her—couldn't help myself. Our relationship developed and got to the point where I had to make a decision: Rosemary, or my family."

Jesus Christ, Dad.

"Your mother had no idea all this was going on," he said, and shrugged. "She was so deep into her depression that she hardly even noticed me. Rosemary, meanwhile, was showing me all kinds of affection, which made my decision easier. I was all set to pack my bags, and then something happened that turned me around—made me realize how stupid I'd been, and how close I'd come to losing it all."

I looked at him, sitting in the Mork chair with his head hanging. The lip of the seat was curled upward, lifting his feet off the floor. He looked like a child.

"Your first word was Mom—or *More*, as you used to say. Niki's was Daddy. And she spoke it so clearly. Her little eyes would light up. Daddy-Daddy. The most perfect sound in the world." He stopped, lifted his head, cracked a sad smile. "First time she said it . . . man, it was like living in a dark house, and suddenly all the windows are thrown open and the light comes streaming in. You feel it on your skin. You taste it. *Inhale* it. I kissed her a thousand times. I kissed your mom. And you, too. Then I got in the car and drove to Rosemary's place. I told her that I'd made my decision—that, in the end, it wasn't even difficult: I was staying with my family."

Dad looked at the blue ceiling. He was silent for a long time, but he hadn't quite finished. There was something beneath the confession. I could sense it bubbling away. A deeper guilt. He shook his head and picked his cuticles, indicating how nervous he was. When he lowered his gaze, twin tears spilled from his eyes and rolled down his cheeks, the same shape, the same speed.

"So that was that. Rosemary went her way—hating me—and I went mine." He ran one sleeve across his face, childlike again, then went back to picking his cuticles. "I went into denial. Buried the whole affair. Moved on. But ever since your accident I've been having . . . dark thoughts."

I groaned and ran my sand-dry tongue along the backs of my teeth. My jaw jutted. A loose hair tickled my cheek.

"Karma," Dad said. He looked at me and then he broke. I watched it happen, as if in slow motion, his chest shaking, face taut, teeth clenched. He was like a man carrying a thousand items precariously balanced, each depending on the placement of the other, and the moment he dropped one, the rest would fall. It happened. Something inside him crashed. He curled like a leaf and wept out the pain he had carried for so long.

It's tough to see your father crying. The world cracks and never fully heals. No matter how many times you see it . . . never gets easier.

I stayed in my body. Didn't hold him. Didn't want his pain.

"Karma," he said again, wiping his eyes. "I believe in it. Always have. And I wonder if what happened to you is *my* fault—that the universe is paying me back by taking my son. Maybe it's just dark thoughts, but I can't shake the feeling that I'm in some way responsible."

Bullshit, I said. *It doesn't work like that.*

"Not because I fell in love with another woman," Dad said. "But because I never told your mother. We're supposed to share everything, and this is something I've kept from her all these years. It's grown inside me, spreading this . . . this self-*loathing*. But here's the weird thing—what I keep thinking about: I was *going* to tell her. I planned it, Wes. A couple of years ago now. I took her out for a meal, a few glasses of wine. You know, soften her up so I could come clean on the drive home. Just trying to make it as painless as possible. Only I couldn't do it. I reasoned—gutless fucker that I am—that it would be easier to live with my self-loathing, than to live without your mom's trust, and for her to think less of me."

He ran his hands through his hair and took a deep breath that, to me, sounded blessedly clear. No hissing or chafing. No dry skin flaking from his lips.

"So I didn't do it." His mouth tightened and he screwed his eyes shut, as if he'd swallowed something bitter. "Karma, Wes; the very next day we got the call about your accident. I couldn't move. Couldn't think. Your mom thought it was grief, and it was, but it was also guilt."

I sighed inside. *Like Grandma's rainbow*, I said to him. *Just coincidence.*

"I have to live with this for the rest of my life," he said. "Even if I tell your mom about Rosemary, I still have to carry this dark thought—this terrible idea that what happened to you was my doing."

Good things happen, Dad, I said. *Bad things, too. That's not karma; it's life.*

"I know you can't hear me, Wes." His eyes flashed from me to the window. Wan light and golden leaves. "But the universe can. And I want it to know that I'm sorry. I've paid more than one man should. Now I just want the pain to go away."

And I could see that pain. The guilt, too. Stacked inside him, strong and tall, like the love inside Niki, the hate inside Wayne. He hopped out of the Mork chair, shuffled to my bedside, took my hand. His tan waistcoat was streaked with tears. He pressed my fingers to his lips. I felt them move as he muttered the word sorry over and over again.

Then he said goodbye.

These final moments—in all likelihood—with my family. Secrets and sins. Love and pain. So many colours. Maybe that's what Grandma Soul meant when she said she was sending me a rainbow. She has always been in tune with spirituality. With the universe. She must have known I'd see sunshine and rain.

Loveable old hippie. I bet if I astral projected to that commune in Florida, she would *feel* me. Chimes would tinkle. She'd grab her guitar and sing, "Aquarius/Let the Sunshine In."

Hub hasn't said goodbye yet. He's paused at the door a few times, debating whether or not to come in, but each time he's carried on walking. Dude can't face it, and

I feel for him, I really do.

Mom's goodbye was the hardest. I'm her little boy, after all. We've always been close, and the bond is *strong*. I thought, for that reason, she would keep it brief: a tearful kiss, and gone. But no, she rode her pain with the strength and fight that I inherited. She brought rainbows.

My eyes are still burning. She blinded me.

"Here," she said, indicating the cradle of her arms. "I held you here when you were seconds old, and kept you there. Never wanted to let you go. You were pure and perfect. My heart ached—it *ached*—with love for you. And still does to this day."

She didn't sit in the Mork chair. She perched on the edge of my bed and curled her hand around mine.

I love you, Mom, I said. *I don't know how long I can keep fighting, but—*

"You've never let me down," she said. "Sure, a little mischievous from time to time, like any boy, but your heart was strong and kind, even at such a young age. I remember you giving up your seat on the bus for an elderly lady. Nobody asked you to. You just did it. Six years old. The lady smiled and sat next to me—whispered in my ear that I'd raised a prince. I almost floated off that bus with pride. But that was you, Westlake. Considerate and caring. It came naturally to you."

Mom didn't look away from me. Not once. Dad had picked his cuticles and stared out the window. Niki had looked out the window, too, and Darryl at his crisp white socks. But Mom's eyes remained fixed on mine.

She didn't cry, either.

She was strong. Unbelievable.

Inspiring.

"You excelled at everything you turned your hand to," she said, brushing hair from my forehead. "So gifted. So determined to succeed. Your enthusiasm was breathtaking, and this may sound strange, but you inspired me to do more, to work harder. I always thought that children should follow the examples set by their parents . . . not the other way around."

Mom wasn't crying, but I can't say the same. My eyes blinked, clicked dryly, but inside I bawled, everything shaking and leaking. Perfect memories cascaded—my every achievement recalled. And for each of them, Mom was there. Dad, too. Both proud, but there was something extra in Mom's expression. A resonance. A shine. Because I grew inside her, and am connected to her in a way I'll never be to Dad. Much as I love him—and it's a *big* love—the bond between mother and child is, at its purest, god-like.

I remember what she'd said to Dr. Thinker when he told her I would be a vegetable for the rest of my life: *I don't believe that.* She'd flapped a hand at my CT scan images, where my brain looked as if it had been flooded with black ink. *My baby is still in there. I can see him. I can feel him.*

She had brushed all the hair from my forehead, but continued to make the motions, drawing her fingers across my brow, behind my ear. So soothing.

I've tried, Mom, I said. My dry eyes clicked again and my Adam's apple bobbed. A stone wrapped in leather. *I've worked so hard, but I just can't find a way out.*

"I was certain you'd find a way out," Mom said, and I felt that invisible line between us glow. I thought it would overheat and break with a little *doink!* sound, like a light bulb blowing. "No doubt in my mind. Because no challenge has ever been too great for you. I kept expecting to come in here one day to find you sitting up in bed, blinking your eyes brightly. And as crazy as it sounds, I *still* think that might happen. It's illogical, I know. Wishful thinking. But I can't get it out of my head."

Her fingers trailed down the side of my face, to my jaw, where the bone pressed against the skin and turned it a bluish colour. She smiled, and where I had seen Niki's love, and Dad's guilt and pain, I saw in Mom an array of emotion. I'm not sure if my superhero power detected it, or if dehydration caused me to hallucinate, but her biofield was overwhelming. Love in abundance, of course. But pride and faith, too. It soaked me. Painted my eyes. I flowed through her, and saw within a wall of impossible strength.

She sat with me for a long time, in silence, stroking my face. I wept and wrapped my soul around her, feeding on her strength as I had in the womb.

I'm going to miss you, Mom.

She kissed my face. My fingers. One after the other.

And I'm scared . . . so scared.

I heard the wind outside—imagined it cold-edged as afternoon tilted to early evening. The perfect soundtrack to my pain. Crows flying through my stomach. The smell of burning in my bones. Scar-pale moon reflecting on my skin. I looked over Mom's shoulder, at a window filled with reddish light, and saw a spiny wing—large as the side of a car—slap against the glass. Dr. Quietus. Ever there. I heard the fire crackle in his chest, my name on every breath, and I clung to Mom as my rag of a body trembled.

"You'll always be with me," Mom said. "I love you, son."

22. Superhero.

I followed him over a course of days. Three or four, I'm not sure, and it's getting hard to think. But I followed him—through crowded bars and along city streets. I watched him swagger and spit and breathe. He drove his APPETITE FOR CONSTRUCTION truck too fast, with the stereo sweating hostile music, and I was right beside him. I read his texts and e-mails. Listened to him on the phone. Watched him workout at Xtreme Couture and jerk off to Internet porn. He shared his anger in a hundred different ways and I gathered it. I was the shiver up his spine.

I followed. And waited.

Yvette had finally come to her senses and dumped his useless ass. The incident with the trophies proved to be the final straw. She collected the broken pieces, set aside what could be fixed, trashed the rest. Then she called Wayne and told him it was over. Her voice was firm and the look in her eye was cool—familiar to me. There was to be no reconciliation. No more chances. Wayne took it badly. Losing a girlfriend he didn't care about wasn't a problem. Being dumped *was*, because—again—it challenged his alpha role. Wayne retaliated the only way he knew how: with cruelty.

U FUCKN BITCH. U THINK I CARE??

DON'T TEXT ME WAYNE. DON'T CALL ME. IT'S OVER.

FUCKN WHORE. WATCH UR BACK.

He went out with the boys and got loaded. Picked a fight at Shoeless Joe's with some dude half his size. Hit a strip club in Mississauga and paid $150 for a blowjob from a Croatian dancer called Mace—saw fit to text Yvette this development: GETTIN M DICK SIKCED NOW. HOW U LIKE TAH??? Yvette blocked his number, but she couldn't block him. He buzzed her apartment at three-twenty in the morning, screaming abuse into the intercom. Yvette cowered in her bed, and he finally took off after one of the neighbours shouted down that the cops had been called.

He tried again the following night, less drunk but equally abusive, and when Yvette didn't buzz him up, he took it out on her car—grabbed a Phillips head screwdriver from his truck and ran it along the driver's side, deeply scoring the yellow paint. Yvette involved the police but couldn't prove that Wayne had caused the damage. They paid him a visit, even so, because they knew that he *had* and they wanted to put a little scare on him, tell him to back the hell off. Wayne told the cops that yeah, he'd kind of lost it and shouted into her intercom, but he didn't damage her car, for Christ's sake, he would *never* do such a thing. They didn't buy his bullshit, but all they could do was warn him to stay away. The next day, Wayne followed Yvette in his truck—tailgating her, grinning behind the wheel. Yvette had been driving to the gym, but when she turned right instead of left on Markham Avenue, and started leading

Wayne toward the O.P.P. detachment, he flipped her the bird and peeled off with a furious blast of the horn. That night Yvette called her mom and made plans to move back to Rouyn-Noranda, while Wayne announced to the world (well, to his sixty-four Facebook friends, at least) that Yvette Sommereux was a blue ribbon cuntstick with chicken tits, and that he was *so fuckn* done with her.

But I wasn't *so fuckn* done with him.

I don't know much about Wayne. I figure there's a reason for his attitude. Maybe he was beaten as a child, or made to feel unloved. Or maybe, like Yvette, he senses something better inside, but is afraid to let it out through fear of rejection. With more time, or inclination, I would have delved into his past. Nobody is born mean, after all. They *become* mean, through circumstance and environment. Who knows . . . maybe I would have cut him some slack if I'd discovered that his mother was a crack whore, or that, as a kid, he'd had his asshole popped by a lecherous uncle. Every supervillain has a backstory. Orphaned, betrayed, haunted, or disfigured. There's always something that draws them to the Dark Side. But whatever happened to Wayne will remain a mystery, and I'm cool with that. I carried his hate and anger inside me, after all. I know how real it is.

Also, I was hell-bent on revenge. I didn't want anything to diminish that.

And nothing did.

I've mentioned the biofield several times—more commonly known as the aura: a wave of energy that surrounds all living organisms. Sounds like something my grandma would experience during a peyote jaunt. Throw in one of her rainbows. Couple of unicorns. Spin a Grateful Dead track and away you go. But it's not like that at all. There's science at work, and it runs deep. Not all scientists would agree with that statement, I know, but to hell with them. I'm smarter, anyway.

It was called the Vital Force in seventeenth-century Europe. You may also know it by its Chinese name, Chi, or its Indian name, Prana. Whatever you call it, the principle is the same: in the simplest, most accurate terms, the biofield is a vibratory signature unique to the cell or molecule it represents. Think of it as a cosmic fingerprint. Every living organism has one, and no two are the same.

It resonates, this fingerprint. And it is possible, through understanding (and certainly with a mind like mine), to recognize and replicate this resonance. It's like two musical notes tuned to the same key, becoming one concordant sound. Once this link is established, energetic signatures can be transferred—through aspects of quantum entanglement and Sheldrake's morphic fields— from one system to another.

In other words, I could resonate with Wayne's biofield, and interact with it. So all the hate and anger I'd collected from him could be transferred back in one brutal hit.

Which is exactly what I did.

That wall of hate came crashing down. I crushed him beneath it.

He left the club just after midnight. Walked rain-washed streets to his truck. I trailed just behind—a weary ghost, laden with the anger I had gathered. The streetlights swam in puddles on the sidewalk. Pools of neon from the Chinese restaurants on Spadina. He bumped into an old man carrying a bundle of newspapers. Didn't apologize. Kicked a garbage can. Hovered for a moment outside a restaurant where Han folk music warbled from a speaker above the door, then stepped inside to grab something from the takeout menu.

Clouds stirred overhead, throwing a little rain, a little thunder.

"Spring roll."

"Number six, yeah?"

"I dunno. Spring fucking roll."

I floated outside, my shoulders aching under the weight of Wayne's anger. That wasn't all, of course. Knowing I was down to my final few days, facing my broken family, *still* searching for a way out . . . I felt so weak. At least I had this, my heroic revenge on Wayne the Fucktard. One last trophy for my Wall of Achievement. My only regret was that he wouldn't see me. I wanted him to look into my eyes as I returned every fat block of animosity.

Wayne got his spring roll and ate it on the move. It was gone in three man-sized bites, oils dribbling down his chin. He balled the trash, dropped it on the sidewalk, and crossed the street. There was an alleyway leading to the Green P where he'd parked. He started down it, weaving a little. I moved ahead of him. Got ready.

I had no idea what to expect. To interact with his biofield so violently . . . would he shudder, as if someone had walked over his grave? Would he fall to the ground, clutching his heart, eyes bulging? He veered toward me, muttering under his breath. The alleyway was illuminated by a streetlight at either end, and featureless, save for a couple of dumpsters and a fire escape snaking to the roof of the building on the right. I waited until he was halfway along, where the shadows were deepest, and then made my move.

I threw my arms wide and let him pass through me, analyzing the vibratory pattern of his biofield, a thing that writhed and kicked. I applied an identical signature to all the hate and anger I had drawn from him over the weeks, and transferred it with a fierce mental push. As much as I could unload in one hit.

Every sneer and unkind word. The birds he'd flipped. His bullish ways and arrogance. Breaking Yvette's trophies. Running a screwdriver along the side of her pretty yellow car. His thick hand around her throat. The bruises on her arms. Punching her in the eye.

Motherfucker.

Punching her in the eye.

I gave it all back to him . . . the way he made everybody— not just Yvette—feel. A massive gulp of his own medicine.

He broke—folded—as if someone had thumped him in the stomach. A wail escaped him and he turned his face to the sky. Fingers hooked. Shaking his head. I took a step back. I knew he'd feel something, but this . . .

This was good.

My turn to sneer.

This is how you make other people feel, Wayne, I said. *Not so cool, huh?*

He sobbed, covered his face with his hands, fell to his knees.

You're a bully. With a heart like nothing. I towered over him, my emotion on fire. All of my frustration and sadness. My fear and determination. A mountain of everything I had been through. Anger, too, that life was wasted on someone like Wayne, who could love but chose not to, who could make a difference but didn't care. *If there's good in you, I can't see it. But I know now just how insecure you are . . . and how sad.*

"No," he moaned. The rain pattered off his shaved head. "Jesus God, no."

I should have left him to his misery, but the anger burned inside me. Wasn't fair that he could move and *live* when I—who had *so* much more to offer—was down to my last breaths. A cloud of resentment stained my energy, my judgement. I threw yet more hate at him, grabbing the bricks I had collected and slamming them into his biofield. I could almost hear the thud as the signature aligned.

He shuddered and crawled away from me, trying to protect himself. It was like running from his own shadow. He collapsed against a dumpster, curled into a ball, and I continued to unload.

"No . . . please, Jesus . . . *please* . . ."

So much anger and aggression, cloaking deeper issues that were surfacing now: his fear of rejection and powerlessness; isolation and sadness. Dude was having an emotional breakdown. A bad one, years in the making. I didn't let up. One brick after another, until my work was done.

I've got no pity for you, I said. *You've got problems, brother. You need to get your shit together.*

He punched the side of the dumpster and dragged himself to his feet. His eyes were wide and scared. I started to float away from him. I had more work to do in the motor cortex, and damn I was weary—didn't want to use any more energy on Wayne. A rumbling sound stopped me.

Thunder, I thought, looking at the stone-coloured sky. But no; I turned around and saw Wayne rolling the dumpster down the alleyway. Its steel body scraped the wall and boomed.

The hell are you doing, Wayne?

It quickly became evident, and I realized I had underestimated his anger, the emotions it masked, and the impact of throwing it all back at him.

Wayne rolled the dumpster to where the fire escape was bolted to the wall and used it to hoist himself onto the lower platform. I watched as he thudded up the stairs, taking them three at a time, moving from one platform to the next with alarming purposefulness. He clearly wanted to act before he could change his mind, and within moments was climbing the short ladder to the roof. He wiped his eyes and veered across the rooftop, muttering denials and apologies that were lost to the wind.

I followed, the city lights shining through me, feeling my physical body rattle and bleed. I needed to return, but this was something I couldn't look away from, any more than I could look away from a helicopter spinning out of control, or a train hurtling toward a collapsed bridge. I was fascinated. Was he going to leap to his death, or was this a cry for help? Either way, I had brought him here. I had done this.

Wayne reached the edge of the rooftop. Stepped onto the ledge. Sixty-five feet above Spadina Avenue.

Do it, I thought, a line straight out of Dr. Quietus's script. I hated that I'd had such a dark thought, but it was easy to remember the bruise beneath Yvette's eye. The way she had sobbed into countless scrunched Kleenex while

Alicia Keys sang—delightfully appropriate now—"Fallin'." Sad but true: a world without Wayne wouldn't be missing much. Do the whole *It's a Wonderful Life* routine, and folk'd be happier.

The rain picked up, falling in grey lines that veiled the city. The skyline was a switchboard of blinking lights in the east, with the top of the CN Tower lost in a swag of cloud. Thunder ripped. A callous gust that made everything swirl, including Wayne. He teetered on the edge. Almost fell.

Could I stop him from jumping? Did I want to?

He leaned forward. I thought he was going and my instinct was to grab the back of his jacket, pull him back, even though I knew my hand would pass right through. But he held himself, an inch—no more—from plummeting to the sidewalk. The rain bounced off his broad shoulders. Ran down his face with the tears.

Do it. That thought again, like Dr. Quietus working through me. I pushed it away and floated closer to Wayne. Below us, the glow of traffic on Spadina Avenue. Neon fading as restaurants closed for the night. A couple, hand in hand, hurrying to get out of the rain. Nobody noticed Wayne, as veiled as the skyline. First anybody would know would be his broken body bleeding into the gutter.

This wasn't a cry for help. I'd crushed him beneath a wall of his own misery. Dude was going to jump.

He muttered something. I don't know what. It was drowned by the rain, by the tears in his throat. His right leg twitched, about to step into emptiness. I knew that all I had to do to send him over was throw another brick at him. Not even a brick. A stone. A pebble. It would send ripples through his biofield and he would be gone.

But who was I to drop the hammer? My life had been ripped from me. I knew its power and beauty. I knew that, for all the universe, only death was bigger. I let go of the anger inside me. Some of it Wayne's. Most of it mine. Ghosted out above the drop, faced him, and then flowed through him. I found a fragment of hope and threw it back at him. It was enough. He stepped back off the ledge and slumped to his knees, wrapped himself into a shape that seemed too small. A world away from machismo. The alpha role was dead. I left him, crying on the rooftop, contemplating a life without anger. I drifted back to the groovy room, where I shook uncontrollably and stared, pale-eyed, at the ceiling.

Where Dr. Quietus spread his wings.

Laughed like he had a shoal of insane people hiding beneath his dark robes.

And took me.

23. SUPERVILLAIN.

I was dragged into a world that reminded me of a movie set. The location for the thrilling finale. An abandoned factory with banks of dusty machinery—drills, saws, and presses—waiting to whir into life. Vats of corrosive substances. Steel catwalks. Chains hanging from the ceiling. The air smelled of oil and burned metal. I looked around, expecting to hear the cinematic score—tension ramped up by the high notes on a piano. Maybe a long, ominous tone lured from a cello. Something fluttered in the partial lighting and I jumped. A butterfly with burning orange wings that had found a way in but couldn't find a way out. It flickered out of sight, lost in the darkness at the far end of the factory.

So this was it. Our final battle.

I couldn't see him, but knew he was there. Crouched high up on the catwalk, or behind one of the machines. Or perhaps he *was* a machine. He'd open his eyes and lights would flash. The motor would start, the conveyor would roll, and I'd be sucked in and chewed up, spat out at the other end in grisly red pieces. I felt like one of the kids in

A Nightmare on Elm Street. Jesus, I was even wearing my pyjamas. Not exactly becoming of a superhero. No cape. No dandy boots. I'd never felt so powerless. I tried to fly; if I could reach the catwalk, I'd have a better view of the factory floor, perhaps anticipate his attack. I hovered three feet above the ground—could go no higher—and came down with a thud.

This wasn't looking good.

A sound from up ahead: scratching, followed by a crunch, like a ball-peen hammer striking bone. I peered through the gloom and saw him, low to the ground, shoulders rounded. He'd dropped from the ceiling, where he'd clung like a spider. I took a step back as he rose to his feet. His wings rippled, black as my fear.

"So this is the end," I said, my voice fragile. I edged away from him, but he took a huge, booming step forward and covered more than half the distance between us. The catwalks shook and the chains rattled. I saw fire inside his cowl.

Westlake Soul, he said. He so loved to say my name.

I wondered if I could fight—if I had anything left after being starved for eleven days, and after using so much energy on Wayne. I had always foiled Dr. Quietus, but things were different now.

He spoke my name again and—*THOOMP!*—stomped his foot. Machinery woke. Cranked dials and blinking lights. Everything shuddered, including me. I turned and ran, weaving between incinerators and spinning saw blades. No doubt I was in Dr. Quietus's world. A place of fire and smoke, with rattling chains and machines that cut and crushed. I had no control. This was his show. He came after me, swinging his fists. I pushed with everything I had, but how long could I keep going? A bird with two broken wings hopping away from a hungry cat.

You've been running for a long time, Westlake Soul.

And I would *keep* running until he caught me, pinned me down, and finished the job he'd started more than two years ago.

It's almost over. So very close.

I ran through a welding bay lined with hideous sculptures. I tipped one over behind me. It broke into sharp pieces, littering the floor. This slowed Dr. Quietus but didn't stop him. He stumbled and roared, then flapped his oily wings and took to the air. I glanced upward and saw him circling above the catwalk. He cried out and swooped, hands like talons.

You can't get away from me!

He grabbed the back of my pyjama shirt and hoisted me off the ground, worked his wings and took me higher. I kicked and struggled but he held fast, then whipped me around and slammed me into the side of an industrial press.

SPRRAAANNKK!

I felt every bone crack. My ribcage collapsed and my skull split from the middle out, following the sutures, like tearing along the dotted lines.

Dr. Quietus howled and I twitched in his claws, drawing what were surely my final breaths. They felt like fishhooks catching on my lungs. He tossed me away and I tumbled through the air long enough to wonder if I would land on one of the spinning saw blades, or in a vat of sulphuric acid. It was the end, no matter what. I'd been beaten at last. It had been long and hard, but the final blow—the actual moment of death—would be quick as a blink.

Or so I thought.

I landed on the catwalk. A pile of broken pieces. I groaned and flopped onto my back, looked up and saw Dr. Quietus touch down at the other end of the walkway. He folded his wings and stepped toward me.

You used to be more of a challenge. He flickered like polished stone. *Where's the fight, Westlake? Where's the will to live?*

I got to my hands and knees and started to crawl. I recalled how I had once been able to fly away from him, break through walls, jump into the Soulmobile and gun that puppy to a place where the shadows weren't so long. Not anymore. Even crawling hurt. Most superheroes lose their powers at some time or other. They always get them back, though, and resume the duty of kicking ass. Wasn't going to happen to me. This was The End, baby. The Death of Westlake Soul. No chance of being brought back by the Entity, or resurrected in the Kryptonian Regeneration Matrix, like Superman. There wasn't a roomful of comic book dudes waiting to draw me back into existence. My final breath would be exactly that.

Pitiful, Dr. Quietus said, stomping toward me, the catwalk creaking under his weight. *And you used to be so strong. You used to tame the ocean.*

Yes. The fury beneath the board and the exhilaration of controlling it, tempering the most powerful thing known to man, if only for a moment. This feeling . . . I *used* it. I got to my feet and staggered three or four steps before being knocked down again. But Dr. Quietus didn't touch me. Didn't need to. His boot came down on the steel walkway—*BRRROINNGG*—and the vibration was enough to send me sprawling.

I got to my feet again. Staggered on.

Dr. Quietus laughed. I heard his wings catch air and turned around to see him floating high above. Made me think of the butterfly I had seen. I had thought it trapped, but maybe I was wrong. It occurred to me now that it was too natural—too *alive*—to be a part of Dr. Quietus's environment. Which meant that it was a part of mine.

I gazed into the darkness at the far end of the factory, where the insect had disappeared. Had it come to show me the way out? A hole in the wall or ceiling, butterfly-sized, that would give me another shot at life, however frail?

It was my only hope.

I grasped the catwalk's rails and pushed on.

That's it, Westlake, Dr. Quietus said. He swooped and perched on the catwalk ahead of me. Head low, oozing smoke. *Keep pushing. Keep fighting, Oh, my bleeding heart!* He took wing again, through a curtain of steam, out of sight. I heard him laughing. Wild sound that wanted to break me.

There was still so far to go, and Dr. Quietus was playing with me—drawing out his pleasure, my pain. The urge to concede was consuming, but I didn't. I worked *harder*, through the suffering, one agonizing step at a time.

The end of the world, Westlake. He swept beneath the catwalk, his wings tight and muscular, then up and out of sight again.

Sweat boiled from my body. My pyjamas clung to my skin, heavy and smeared with oil. I licked my lips, taking moisture that rolled down my throat like ice (and back in the groovy room I groaned, devoid of moisture for so long). I pressed on—could now see the factory's back wall. No sign of any frailties, but there was the butterfly, as bright as a flame, tacked to the underside of a rafter.

Get me out of here, I said, and it fluttered, orange wings ticking, to another rafter closer to the corner.

I gathered strength from somewhere and shuffled faster—hell, it was almost a run. The catwalk was coming to an end, though, and I still had at least thirty feet to go. Below me: conveyors and pistons, clouds of steams, cogs turning. It was a loud world, everything grinding, wheezing. I looked for Dr. Quietus and saw him crouched on an oversized engine that coughed toxins. He pointed at me, wreathed in smoke.

What are you going to do, surfer boy?

I looked at the distance between the end of the catwalk and the butterfly. Pipes hissing. Chains hanging. A conveyor loaded with scrap metal, chugging toward a crusher with a throat like a black hole.

It's over, Dr. Quietus said. He leapt from the engine and spread his wings. I lost him for a second as he meshed with the darkness, then he was on me, striking hard and fast. No time to react. His boot connected with my chest and lifted me clear off the walkway.

KA-WHUNK!

I spilled over the edge and fell to the conveyor below, so close to being impaled on an ugly jag of steel. I screamed and puked blood. Tried to move but the pain was unimaginable. The conveyor rumbled and through the tears in my eyes I saw the crusher, less than twenty feet away, swallowing snarls of metal and spitting out perfect cubes.

Dr. Quietus whirled above me, howling triumphantly, then touched down on the conveyor and planted his boot on my chest.

And in the end, he said, *you die, just like the rest of them— the millions of heroes who have come before. You're not so special.*

I screamed again, spraying blood from the back of my throat, teeth stained red. With huge effort, I grabbed Dr. Quietus's boot and tried to lift it from my chest. He shook his head and tensed the muscles in his leg, exerting more pressure.

I don't think so, he said.

The conveyor rumbled on. I heard the crusher sucking in ugly chunks of metal, smashing its jaws. Twelve feet away. Eleven.

Your final seconds, Dr. Quietus growled. His smile was a blackened grille, too wide, too hungry. *And you get to spend them with me. How delightful.*

He threw back his head and laughed in true supervillain style.

A bead of orange in the corner of my eye. The butterfly, still on the rafter. I was moving toward it. A flicker of hope . . .

The end, Dr. Quietus said.

Not yet, I said. I reached behind me and grabbed the first thing my hand happened upon: a stone-sized lump of iron. I curled my fingers around it, twisted my body, and threw with insane sidearm precision. It hurtled toward Dr. Quietus like a tiny asteroid, disappeared inside his cowl, and bounced hard off that black-grille mouth.

PWAAANNG!

He cried out and spilled backward, arms pinwheeling. I didn't waste a second in following up. I sprang to my feet in one lithe movement, strutted forward, then dropkicked the son of a bitch.

KAROOOMPHH!

He crashed into the scrap pile on the belt behind him, scattering it all before falling to the ground ten feet below. I knew he'd be back on his feet in no time. I had to move, and quickly. One shot at escape, to buy—*maybe*—one more day. I spat yet more blood and looked at the crusher. So close now.

Dr. Quietus roared. He worked his wings and sent chunks of scrap metal spinning in all directions. Fists clenched, bleeding oil and anger, he came at me again.

I lurched, not away from, but toward the crusher. I planted the sole of my foot on a tangle of junk and used it to launch myself—flew through the air for a heartbeat before starting to descend. Below me, the junk I had launched from toppled into the machine and I heard the jaws do their thing.

You resilient little cocksucker! Dr. Quietus screamed.

I swallowed blood and wept—reached out, and managed to grab one of the chains hanging from the ceiling. It jerked in my hand but I held on, kicked my legs and swung high. Over the crusher. Through a screen of blue sparks. I let go of the chain and grabbed another, like Tarzan swinging on vines, and took this one all the way to the rafters.

Okay, I said to the butterfly. *I'm here. Let's book it.*

The butterfly opened its wings, fluttered to the exit (the thinnest seam between the wall and ceiling), and disappeared. I imagined it suddenly rising into the clean sky outside my bedroom window, above a world turning gold. I lunged after it, crying out . . . almost reached the gap when I felt Dr. Quietus's hand curl around my ankle. He pulled hard—jerked me back.

Not so fast, pretty boy.

I clung to the rafter with everything I had, fingernails scraping along the cold metal. I was so close to the gap that I could see a thread of Surf City Blue. Smell coffee and waffles. Hear the radio playing. Dr. Quietus's hand tightened on my ankle. I twisted around and kicked with my other foot. It connected with the dark oval of his face. It felt like stomping on a bed of cockroaches that clicked and scratched against my skin. I kicked him again . . . again. He roared, lost his grip, slumped back.

I hit that seam of light like a dart.

My eyes snapped open.

The groovy room was cool and bright. Altogether beautiful. My dry body trembled and I exhaled air that I was sure would smell of sulphur and sweat.

Jesus, I gasped. *Jesus Christ.*

That was it. I had nothing—*nothing*—left. The next fight would be my last. Judging from the way I'd pissed off Dr. Quietus (I'd *dropkicked* him, for the love of God), I had a feeling he'd be returning soon. Probably before the end of the day.

It's over, I said.

Yeah, a sad voice agreed, so soft I barely heard.

My gaze rolled by chance to the doorway, and there was Hub. My dog. My best friend. He tried to smile, but I could see that his eyes were big and moist.

Hey, I said weakly.

He closed his eyes and his mouth trembled as he whined.

Dude had finally come to say goodbye.

24. Downward Dog.

So much sadness, huh? And so many tears. I've tried to keep things upbeat here. Not exactly easy. Believe me, it would rock my socks to be able to tell you how goddamn happy everybody is. Just singing and dancing, like the Ewoks at the end of *Jedi*. Can't do it, though. I have to tell it like it is.

My tragic life.

Here's the thing: roll back the clock to any time before my accident, and there wouldn't be tears. Or so few as not to matter. We were always laughing, goofing off. Sure, we had our ups and downs, like any family. Arguments and slammed doors. Then there was Mom's postpartum depression (which I didn't even know about until Dad told me). But the rough times didn't last, and for the most part ours was a household of smiles. Those days are history. The stuff of memories and old home movies.

It's crazy how one moment—one decision—can change so much.

Scary, too.

It'd be cool to fast-forward three or four years. You'd see

a family rebuilt and smiling again. Niki with (if she works her ass off) a university degree and a steady boyfriend, planning the rest of her life. The groovy room turned into a mini gym, or maybe a study. Hub still rocking it, but with a little grey in his snout. Dad and Mom dancing most nights. The only reminder of the son and brother they had lost would be an oil painting on the living room wall, a reproduction of one of my surfing photos—tearing through the glasshouse at Banzai Pipeline, perhaps, lovingly recreated with an impressionist's flare.

Yeah . . . that'd be cool.

I'm a sucker for a happy ending, so let's just do it now: *And they all—except for Westlake, who died—lived Happily Ever After . . . eventually.*

There.

But prior to this joyous conclusion . . .

You son of a bitch, Hub said, and I thought that was kind of rich, coming from him. *You said you were going to get better. Dude, you promised.*

I nodded inside and willed my eyes to roll away from him, and by pure fluke they did. Not completely, but enough that I didn't have to look at his sad little face. I'd been waiting for him to come speak to me—was pissed that he hadn't, to be honest, and now that he was here, I couldn't stand to look him in the eye. My chest hitched. A leaking sound escaped my mouth. Sounds crazy, but I almost wished I could be back in that factory with Dr. Quietus. Saying goodbye to Hub was going to be just as hard.

He came a little farther into the room, stopped short of my bed. I thought of the many times he had dropped into a sun patch or curled next to the Mork chair. Preferred spots for our conversations. Not today, though. This wasn't going to be a leisurely chinfest. He growled with displeasure and gave his tail an agitated flick. I felt his eyes boring into me.

So, what's the deal? he asked.

The deal?

Yeah. Are you just giving up? His paws tapped on the hardwood as he stepped closer. *The end. Game over. That's it, huh?*

Dude, I said. *I've tried so hard.*

You've tried everything?

My eyes rolled back to him. *I've got nothing left*, I said.

Hub lowered his head and was silent for a long time. Then he whined, ears pinned low, and surprised me by jumping onto my bed. He looked at my useless body, skin chafed and pink, hollow stomach fluttering. It looked as if the bedsheets had been laid over a pile of broken sticks. The pressure of his weight on the bed—all of what, twenty-five pounds?—sent pain pulses through my legs and lower back. It hurt so much and I braced inside, but I didn't want him to jump down. Not for anything.

You can't give up, Hub said, and his mouth turned a sad smile. *There are still waves to surf.*

Yeah, bitchin' waves, I agreed. *I'll surf them in my dreams.*

Come on, man. You're stronger than that.

I'm beat, Hub. It's over.

He came closer. The movement sent spikes through my pelvis and ribs. My legs flared as if they had been dipped in oil and set to burn. Yet, if I could, I would have pulled Hub closer still, hugged him tight to my chest, buried my face in his golden fur. I think he sensed this, because he—so gently—edged forward, into the gap between my arm and my side, and rested his head on the ridge of my thigh.

This is breaking my heart, Wes.

I know, brother.

Don't know what I'm going to do without you.

There's so much love here. You'll be fine.

Won't be the same, dude. He closed his moist eyes. *That's all I'm saying.*

I had nothing to say to that. We were trying to encourage each other, but it was so hard. The truth—that I probably wouldn't live to see the sun go down—was too vast a thing to overcome. Encouragement splintered like ice and we fell into our own freezing pools. Hub whimpered. I groaned. He nuzzled against my side and a muscle in my forearm flexed weakly.

I'm going to miss you, he said.

More silence, and I took it—enjoyed Hub's company while I still could, reflecting on better days. I remembered when we got him from the animal shelter, how he'd been reclining in his cage with one foreleg covering his eyes, little pink belly showing. Countless walks and outings, through meadows and forests, along river banks. Rabbits springing, whitetail bounding through the high grass, and Hub just as chill as can be. Hanging on the patio at Turtle Jack's, Hub with a bowl of water, me with a bottle of Rickard's Red, doing our thing and wooing the ladies. And hours spent at the Beaches, listening to The Edge on a retro boom box, watching the sun rip pink patterns on Lake Ontario.

Good times.

I'm going to miss you, too, I said.

I heard my family eating breakfast in the kitchen. The clash of their cutlery. The waffle iron sizzling second and third helpings (the smell of the batter, rich and full of fat, made my empty stomach cry). They ate in silence, the radio playing soft sounds behind them, and I wondered if they sensed—as I did, and Hub—that this was the day. One final round of tears, and then time for healing.

I'm not giving up on you, Hub said. *Just so you know.*

I appreciate that, I said. *Wish to hell I could reward that faith.*

My acute canine senses tell me you've got one gnarly trick left in you. Hub tried to smile and I wrapped myself around him. So much love. I didn't ask him where those senses were during the days of tension, when Fat Annie quit and Mom and Dad had deliberated over their decision. "Acute" was not an adjective that sprang to mind. But then, I hadn't exactly been quick to catch on, either.

There's a wave coming, Hub continued. *A real bomb—*

Like the one that got me into this mess?

Bigger, dude. And you're climbing the face quickly. Looks like you're going to wipeout, but if you can attack the lip at just the right moment, pull some insane aerial—a rodeo flip, or something—there's a chance you can gain control and ride it out.

A sweet analogy, but grounded in make-believe. Hub knew it, too. He wouldn't have spent the last two weeks moping around if he truly believed I had any chance of pulling one last trick. We knew the reality: the bomb had already hit. Smashed my body against the rocks and tossed me to the shore. But Hub was doing his best to encourage me . . . to throw a little light into my final hours.

Love my dog. Yes, I do.

Tell me you'll try, he said.

But there was nothing *to* try. Everything had failed on me. I was falling fast, out of control. Still, I couldn't let Hub shine the light on his own.

Hey, I said. *I haven't backed down from a wave yet.*

He gave his tail a loose thump, but it was impossible to read the emotion in it. Settled his chin on my upper leg and closed his eyes. My breath rattled. I rode the pain. Out in the kitchen, Mom, Dad, and Niki packed away their breakfast things, clattering dishes and cutlery, but still not speaking.

You'd better hustle, I said to Hub, *if you want to snag some leftover waffles.*

Forget that, Hub replied. His lips flapped as he sighed. *I've been away too long. I'm staying right here with you, brother.*

I felt his light. His miniature sun.

You're the best friend ever, I said.

Always loved you, man, he said. *Always will.*

I rolled into fragile sleep, but not for long. When I woke, I saw that Hub was sleeping, too, in almost the same position, except he'd flipped onto his side and had one foreleg curiously cocked in the air. I looked at him for a moment, wondering what dreams chased through his mind. Easy to imagine them full of love, set in a world that was bigger from his perspective. Perhaps he ran beside me as I skateboarded the smoothest sidewalk, beneath the bluest sky. Or maybe he was back at the Beaches, paws buried in the sand, feeling the wind in his fur and looking at a lake that stretched as far as he dared to hope.

My arm jerked. Hub snapped awake but my hand, by chance, came down on his side.

It's okay, dude, I said. *Keep sleeping. It's cool.*

He settled down again, closed his eyes. My fingers flexed against the bow of his ribcage and I felt his heart running like it would never stop.

25. THE BEAUTY
AND THE BIRD.

Yeah, they sensed it, all right. Mom and Dad had taken time off work, and Niki hadn't gone to school. By mid-morning they were taking turns checking on me, which amounted to little more than poking their heads around the door. I was too tired to analyze their expressions. They appeared at once relieved and exasperated that I was still drawing breath. I thought Mom would shoo Hub away, maybe plant her foot in his ass when she saw him snuggled in the crook of my arm. But she didn't. She merely covered her mouth with one hand and called for Dad and Niki to come see. They all stood in the doorway, looking at us with—you guessed it—tears in their eyes.

"He knows," Mom said. "Dogs are so sensitive."

"Psychic, too," Niki said. "I saw it on TV."

"It's true," Dad confirmed.

Hub and I lay there while the minutes ticked away and the death checks continued, Hub dozing, occasionally waking and snuggling a little closer, and me looking at the ceiling, or at my Wall of Achievement if my head happened to flop that way. I drifted out of body a few times for a change of scenery. Didn't go far. The living room. The kitchen. Could have released anywhere, of course—perched on the moon, or rode wild horses on Sable Island—but I wanted to spend my final hours at home. Besides, Yvette was due around lunchtime. Probably my last chance to see her. To feel her touch.

Conversation remained strained, although it got a little heated when Dad suggested taking me out for a drive. He reasoned that I shouldn't spend my last day in a box, and that everybody's energy would benefit from a more appealing environment.

"Westlake is not aware of his surroundings," Mom said. "It doesn't make a difference where he is."

"Makes a difference to me," Dad said. "I would feel better—energetically—if I could take him for a walk along the river, or drive north to some beautiful, peaceful lake and lay him down beside it."

"I understand," Mom said. She stroked Dad's face. It was the first time I had seen them touch since they danced to "Famous Blue Raincoat," and it made my heart work just a little faster. "You're wonderful, Cedar. A sweet, sweet man. But it's not practical. And, if you're honest with yourself, it's more for your benefit than Westlake's."

"Of course," Dad replied. "But not *only* for my benefit, for all of ours. Just imagine . . . surrounded by trees, a tranquil lake, the sun going down as Westlake slips away. It could be a real spiritual moment. No less than he deserves."

"I think it could be more traumatic than spiritual," Mom opined. "I mean, what if he dies in the car?"

"Ewww," Niki offered.

"We won't go far," Dad said.

"Okay, you really need to get this idea out of your head," Mom said. "It's romantic and foolish, and it has nothing to do with Westlake. Besides, we don't know for sure that he will die today. What are you going to do if he doesn't? Throw him in the car and try again tomorrow?"

"I just want to do something special," Dad said.

"But for all the wrong reasons," Mom said. "We're all feeling guilty, Cedar. Find another way to deal with it."

They exchanged more words, Dad's voice climbing an octave, doing the Mickey Mouse thing, proof that he was agitated—either because Mom had shot down his idea, or because she had called out his motive: guilt. In the end they compromised: I'd get an hour in the garden, not on the deck but on the grass, facing the maples.

"It's not exactly Algonquin Park," Dad said. "But it'll do."

Yvette arrived just before midday. Hub's ears pricked up when he heard her car pull into the driveway, but he didn't leave my side. No excited yapping in the hallway or running around in circles, like he used to. She looked incredible, too. She'd dyed her hair blonde and cut it shorter. Had some rouge in her cheeks. A tiny diamond nose-stud. I couldn't remember if I'd seen that before, or if it was something new. Best of all, she looked freer . . . *lighter*. Kicking Wayne out of her life was the healthiest thing she'd done in a long time. The dude was history and she was beginning to shine again. I was delighted to see it. More beautiful than Algonquin Park. Even in the fall.

She had coffee with my parents and they discussed the likelihood of this being my last day. The conversation progressed to my funeral. Mom plucked Kleenex and invited Yvette, told her that white lilies were the flower of choice. Dad said they'd arranged for surfboard-shaped wreaths (*très* cool), and for Joe Strummer's version of "Redemption Song" to be played at the service (*très* cooler). Then he and Mom had an up-tempo discussion about my ashes. Dad wanted to fly to BC and scatter them in the ocean. Mom wanted to keep them closer to home. She suggested burying them in the garden, but Dad was afraid that Hub—being so close to me—would dig them up. Maybe even eat them.

All this time I floated around Yvette, soaking in her radiance. Along with the many other emotions bounding through me, I felt a tremendous sense of pride. In Yvette, of course, but in myself, too. I'd taken care of Wayne (she would never know how close he came to taking a nosedive off a seven-storey building in downtown Toronto), but more importantly, I'd inspired her to create her own Wall of Achievement, and to rediscover the value and strength that Wayne's abuse had taken from her. Not bad for a guy who can't even wiggle his toes.

Yvette had inspired me, too. Let's not forget that. She made me feel good . . . *normal*, almost. And when down—which was often—I recalled her face and picked myself up. Fought harder.

She was a superhero, too. Sif to my Thor.

And she wasn't done yet.

She came into my room and our connection was immediate, amplified. Perhaps because we both knew this was the last time we would be together. I swear to God, if you'd pulled the blinds and shone a black light into the room, you would have seen something sizzling between us. Charged air.

I said to Hub, *Dude, give us five.*

Hub didn't protest, but I could tell wasn't happy about leaving my side. He blinked sleepy eyes, jumped down from the bed, and reluctantly shuffled from the room.

Well, I said to Yvette, and tried to tip a wink. *Just the two of us, huh?*

She looked at me for a while, saying nothing, the air crackling between us. Her nose-stud caught the light and winked rhythmically. I wished I could tell her how pretty she looked. How the blonde complimented her blue/green eyes. To speak the words out loud, so she could hear them. Without doubt.

"Okay," she said, and closed the door—something she'd never done before, effectively shutting out my family. She may as well have hung a "Do Not Disturb" sign outside.

Why the privacy? I asked.

She stepped toward my bed and I felt a chill run through me. Didn't like it at all. I liked the accompanying thought even less: Yvette grabbing one of my pillows and smothering me with it, ending this for everybody, finishing the job she'd started when she unplugged my PEG tube. The twist in the tale: she wasn't a trained healthcare professional at all, but a dark accomplice to Dr. Quietus. She'd steal the last few beats of my heart, then rip off her pretty mask to reveal a bone-face crawling with maggots and spiders. Wings would unfurl from between her shoulders, and with a single muscular movement she'd break through the window and join her wicked lover in the sky.

Yvette Sommereux AKA *Mademoiselle La Mort*.

This crazy idea tumbled from my mind the moment she smiled. Gone. Like it had never been there.

"I wanted to thank you," she said.

Thank me? I said, frowning. Not that she could tell. I looked like a cracked mannequin.

"Just for being who you are," she said, and leaned close to me. As always, I could smell the coconut in her hair. And something new: the faintest trace of ammonia from the dye, and the fragrance of a different soap. She touched my face, then pulled back the top sheet, revealing a body of loose pieces.

I don't know how to be anybody else, I said. Everything inside me reached for her. *I am Westlake Soul.*

She smiled again—left my side, only for a moment, to assemble what she needed for my bed bath. Care to the very end. I heard her in the bathroom, filling bowls with warm water, opening cabinets for soap, towels, sponges. She wheeled everything out on a cart and started to undress me. Careful hands removed my pyjama shirt, tilting my body to minimize stress. Still hurt like hell, but I didn't care. Her fingers trailed along my chest, my shoulders. Sometimes you have to take the rough with the smooth.

"There's something about you, Westlake," she said. "I can't quite put my finger on it. But when I've needed strength—particularly lately, with everything that's been going on—I've thought of you . . . the mark you've left on people in such a short time, the things you've achieved, the love you've given, and the love you'll leave behind."

Off came my pyjama bottoms. She gently rolled my hips and was able to slide them down without causing too much pain. My diaper followed. Just a few drops of blood today. She tucked it into a tight ball and dropped it in the genie.

"Maybe it's because you didn't get the chance to make

mistakes and hurt people." She folded a few towels and placed them beneath me to absorb the runoff. "But to me you represent everything that is good and right, and you came into my life when I needed you most. I've drawn so much strength from you."

I didn't want to miss her touch, but I left my body for just a moment, pressed myself against her, felt a wave of something so real that everything else—the brightly painted room, the air, *everything*—seemed fallacious. I inhaled vigorously. Fell back into my body like I'd been dropped by a bullet.

You helped me, too, I said. *You made me reach deeper, believe harder.*

She dipped the sponge into soapy water and began washing my upper arms and shoulders. Spores of dead skin melted away. My toes curled, somewhere between pleasure and pain.

"I used to imagine that we were together," she said with a smile, moving the sponge to my chest. Water pooled in the dip of my breastbone. "Silly maybe, but it got me through some difficult times."

Not silly at all, I said. *I had the same fantasy. Many times over.*

"You found a way to rebuild. We got married and moved to the country. Did the things that married couples do."

Her choice of words intrigued me—set something tumbling through my brain, trying to gain momentum. Maybe it was a Québécoise thing. A quirk in the translation. *You found a way to rebuild*. Not heal. Not get stronger. *Rebuild*.

"I always wanted to be with someone like you. Someone kind. And strong."

How could she not see—through faint and papery skin—my heart beating? A heavy boot locked in my chest, kicking, stomping. I tried to reach out, sail my fingers through her hair, cup the back of her skull, pull her toward me. Water trickled down my sides and that single odd word—*rebuild, rebuild, rebuild*—continued to run childlike through my mind.

She rolled me onto my left side and washed my back. Crisscrossed with cracks. Pitted with sores. So delicate with the sponge. I sighed, my eyelids flickering. She dabbed me dry before easing me onto my back again.

"I prayed for you to get better." She rinsed the sponge and started on my legs. "It happens, you know. Sometimes. I've seen it. A person in a coma or vegetative state, for *years* . . . one day they just open their eyes, and there they are. Back again."

Yeah, I said. *I prayed for that, too.*

"And with rehabilitation and hard work, they are able to get back on track. Maybe not quite the same." She shrugged, lifted my legs, washed the backs of them. "But certainly able to think, to communicate, sometimes even walk. And I always believed that if you were to get better, you'd go all the way."

I tried, I said. *Worked my ass off, baby.*

"I thought you'd be back on that surfboard." She paused, looked at my Wall of Achievement. "Riding those waves."

Yeah, you and me both.

Neither of us spoke while she cleaned my ass. Pink smears on the sponge. She rinsed, patted me dry. Lowered my legs and cleaned my balls.

I know people have found a way out, I said. *It is possible, but I guess I've been doing it all wrong. Couldn't find the right switch to hit, or door to open.*

"It's all feeling . . . instinct. Means nothing." Yvette finished drying me, then took the folded towels from around my body and placed them on the cart. "I would have looked foolish if I'd mentioned this to your parents. Maybe if I'd been working with you a little longer, I could have. But I'm the new girl. I don't know you like they do, and when your mother told me that your life support was to be discontinued, what could I say? Could I question the decision—as hard as it was, with all the years she has known you, and loved you—based on a *feeling*?"

It's okay, I said. *I understand.*

"It would only have caused more pain and confusion."

You're right.

She wheeled the cart into the bathroom, grabbed a fresh diaper, then a clean set of pyjamas from the closet. Pale blue cotton with navy blue piping. It's strange to see the clothes you'll be wearing when you die. The clothes that a mortician—a person you don't know, and will never meet—will strip from your body. Fold neatly and hand back to your next of kin. You almost don't want to put them on.

"But I got to meet you, and care for you, if only for a short while." She lifted my legs again and snapped me into the diaper. The tight polyester pinched my skin. "I wish it could have been different."

Yeah. Me, too, I said. My jaw dropped open, as if one of the pins holding it in place had broken, and my eyes reeled to the window. It had been overcast all week, but now I could see a crack of blue sky. A whisper of sunshine filtering through. *Heghlu'meH QaQ jajvam,* as the Klingons say: Today is a good day to die.

Yvette unfolded my pyjama bottoms, was about to put them on me, but stopped, sat on the edge of my bed, and placed her hand on my chest. She leaned close. Her eyes— her nose-stud—gleamed.

"I'll never forget you, Westlake."

Was she going to kiss me?

"Ever." She leaned closer still. That coconut smell again.

My heart lurched like a dog on a leash, drawn by some shimmery thing.

Why couldn't I have met you before all this? I said, trying to exert the muscles in my neck and push my head forward. I wanted our lips to meet. More than anything. *We could have had all of each other. We could have ruled the world.*

"You changed my life." A little closer. I could smell her breath. A hint of coffee, and something sweeter. Her fingers tensed on my chest and it felt exquisite. Bombs could have exploded around me and I would not have noticed. A wrecking ball could have passed through the house and I would still have been caught in that moment. It was her eyes. I could see her intention in the softening of her eyelids, the alluring sparks of blue and green. I tried to pucker my lips, as you do before a kiss, but my jaw still swung on its broken hinge.

All of each other, I said again.

"Thank you, Westlake," she said, and it happened: she closed the distance between us and her mouth met mine. Full of warmth and sweetness. Our teeth clashed and our noses squished. I felt her fingernails digging into my chest. Her hair tickled my cheek.

No Sleeping Beauty moment. No fairy tale scene. I didn't suddenly wake up, scoop Yvette into my arms, and carry her—bluebirds singing—into a Happy Ever After. I just lay there in my diaper, my skin cracked and my toes curled.

But in that kiss—and it lasted only two seconds—I saw everything that could have been: Yvette holding my hand as I learned to walk again, feeding me solids and wiping my chin. Watching movies together, munching popcorn, laughing and crying at the same things. Concerts at the ACC, dancing like crazy people while everyone around us remained in their seats. Driving a VW camper van cross-country, curtains in the windows and a couple of boards strapped to the roof. Teaching Yvette how to surf just like she taught me how to walk. Vacations in Europe and Asia. Tattoos in Thailand. Summer jobs in Fiji. Apartment hunting in some artsy community close to the water. Children with blue/green eyes and their parents' taste in music. Surfing by day, playing made-up games with seashells by night.

I saw it all in her kiss.

Sunlight streamed through the window. I moaned.

Her mouth closed over my upper lip. Plucked it lightly as she pulled away.

"Thank you," she said again.

There was a knock at the door and Yvette sprang to her feet, grabbed my pyjama bottoms and started to slip them onto my legs. The door opened and Dad looked in.

"Everything okay?"

"Fine," Yvette said coolly, lifting my ass and drawing the PJ bottoms up around my waist. "Wes has had his bath. Just getting him dressed."

"Good," Dad said, stepping into the room. He didn't suspect a thing. I'm not sure what he would've done if he'd caught Yvette kissing me. He'd probably think it both inappropriate, and totally groovy. Yvette gave away nothing in her expression, but I was sure that I looked as guilty as any red-blooded sinner, even though my face hung in the same paralyzed position—a neural reaction to (almost) being caught by my father, linked to memories of childhood misdeeds. Go Team Freud!

"I thought Wes could have a few moments in the garden," Dad said, helping Yvette get me into my pyjama shirt. "The sun just came out. It's beautiful out there."

"Sure," Yvette said, and they lifted me into my chair. Dad grabbed a blanket and wrapped it around me, and like all such actions it struck me as bizarre given that— according to medical science—I couldn't feel anything, including the cold. Yvette gave me a small, knowing smile, and then I was wheeled away from her, through the living room, onto the rear deck. I tried to look back but couldn't, of course—could only pray I'd see her again before she left. One last time.

Dad bumped my chair down the deck steps, cussing colourfully, and pushed me across the lawn. He found an ideal spot beneath a maple with flaming leaves. The sun ran through the branches. Stained me red.

"There you go, baby," he said, and kissed me high on the cheek. "Enjoy."

Love you, Dad, I said, and watched him walk back toward the house, head hanging. He pulled open the back door and Hub—poised on the other side of the glass—tried to shoot through the gap before it was wide enough. He whined and

Dad grinned, then helped him out by pulling the door an inch or two wider. Hub squeezed through, ears cocked, tongue lolling. He followed the tracks my wheels had made on the lawn and joined me beneath the maple.

Couldn't wait to get out here, huh? I asked.

Something like that, Hub replied with a smile. He nuzzled my leg, then turned in a tight circle—like dogs do—and slumped next to my chair.

I was about to tell him that Yvette had kissed me but was distracted by a flash of pain. It burst through me, from the chest outward, and then drew in again. I stiffened in my chair. Dark veins beating in my neck.

Dude! Hub jumped to his feet and looked at me, his ears flat now.

It's okay, I managed. *Just a little pain. Gone now.*

Scared me, man.

Sorry . . . it's . . . yeah, okay . . . gone.

Hub continued to watch as my body relaxed and my head rested against the wheelchair's buffers. Jesus, that hurt. I hissed and my dry eyes clicked. I would have wept if I'd had enough moisture in my body.

I was going to say . . . My chest thumped beneath the blanket. I counted to ten and my breathing steadied. . . . *kissed me.*

What?

She kissed me, dude. Right on the mouth.

Yvette?

Of course Yvette.

You're serious?

Hell to the yeah.

Holy shit, man, that's so dope. Hub's tail jerked and he

showed his teeth. Biggest grin I'd seen from him in a long time. *So how do you feel?*

I brought her kiss to mind once again. Relived it perfectly. Every moment. I could blissfully relive it a thousand times during my final hours, but something else—as red as the leaves—was burning inside me. Something I couldn't ignore.

Like I want more, I said to Hub, drawing on that feeling inside. *Like I want to keep fighting.*

Again I relived her kiss. The muscles in my upper lip twitched.

Yeah, Hub said. He growled and clawed at the grass. *There's the Westlake I know and love. You're going to give it one last shot?*

One last gnarly trick, I said.

A cool breeze hurried through the back garden, making the leaves chatter. I inhaled at just the right moment and filled my body with fresh air. It felt good to be outside, listening to birdsong and distant traffic sounds—people going about their normal lives. I scented bark and grass. The leafy tang of autumn. I breathed it. Cherished it. Loved Dad for getting me out of the groovy room, even if it meant being away from Yvette. The air filled my lungs with fragrance and life. It was just what I needed.

Yvette's kiss pressed at my memory and, though it was tempting, I pushed it away. There'd be a deluge of kisses— and a lot more besides—if I could land this trick. Whatever the trick might be. My eyes closed and I drifted for . . . I don't know how long. Fifteen minutes. Maybe as long as half an hour. I used this time to consider the motor cortex, barren and black, and formulate plans for some kind of mental drilling rig. I could power it with the electrical impulses in my brain, bore deep into the stony ground and hopefully strike . . .

I snapped out of it, my train of thought derailed by the sensation of something moving on top of my head. Something . . . *familiar*. My left eye crept open. Hub was sleeping beside my chair, his tail twitching. I called his name. He did the whuffling thing—his lips puffing out—but didn't wake.

Okay, I said. *So you're back.*

What can I say? Your charm is appealing. I thought I'd drop by and see how you are feeling.

I'm still not sure if this exchange actually happened. I think it more likely a moment of hallucinatory genius. One that cunningly piggybacked a certain memory. Happened to William Blake all the time. Dali, too. Those dudes were drugged out of their skulls, of course, but I was in a great deal of pain. The mind is uncertain at such times. It likes to play tricks. But real or not, the moment had *impact*, and I present it to you here exactly how I saw it.

The goldfinch hopped from one side of my skull to the other, blinking its little black eyes and flicking its feathers.

Bird, I said. *You're spoiling my moment in the sun. Perhaps my last* ever *moment in the sun. So how about—*

It pecked me. Little son of a bitch actually *pecked* me.

Take a chill-pill, it sang, *or I'll just fly away. This time next week I could be in L.A. With sunshine and romance, the Hollywood class. Not perched on the head of an ungrateful ass.*

Ungrateful? I replied. *Not at all. I really appreciate you making me look like a total dick. It's exactly how I want to spend my final moments.*

It shook its feathers and hopped around, as if looking for a comfortable position. I groaned and tried to wake Hub again. A few choice barks and the bird would be gone. But Hub was down deep and not to be roused. Dude was no help at all.

Okay, I said. *I'll ask nicely . . . please, Mr. Goldfinch—*

I came here to help, I'm all about giving. So hear me out, Wes, if you want to keep living.

Help? I said. *You're a frickin' bird. What are you going to do . . . perform miraculous brain surgery with your beak?*

It twittered musical laughter. I felt its tiny talons digging into my scalp.

When you see the world, it chirped knowingly, *from a bird's point of view, you can't help but learn a lesson or two.*

My other eye peeped open and rolled toward the house. I saw Niki in the kitchen fixing herself lunch. Just my luck she'd look out and see me. OMG. Grab her cell phone and take more snaps for her Facebook album. Westlake and the Bird Part II. LM-Fucking-AO. She'd call Mom and Dad and—Oh, Jesus!—Yvette, too. They'd all come outside and laugh their asses off. I bet even Hub would wake up and start laughing. *Sorry, dude*, he'd say. *But that's some funny shit.*

I didn't want to be laughed at. I wanted them to see me standing, walking, talking. I wanted to be strong again.

You can help me? I asked the bird.

Yes, Wes, it replied, bobbing its head.

Help me to heal? To get better?

There's more to healing than hoping and kissing. The thing you most need is the one thing you're missing.

That's genius, I said bitterly. *So what do I need?*

The goldfinch hopped and fluttered its wings. *It has to*

be strong and it has to be tall. Explore human nature and build a new wall.

Is that all . . . a wall?

Jesus.

The Wall of the Self, built with love, hate, and sin. Kindness and fear, and throw some pride in. Sympathy, sadness, excitement, and greed . . . all of the things that you humans need.

And with that the little bird took wing, flying upward through the branches. It disturbed the leaves and one of them broke away, spiralled slowly down to land on my shoulder. Another leaf fell. Then a third. This one seesawed onto the tip of Hub's nose. He spluttered and jerked awake, snapping at nothing.

Whafuck?

Just a leaf, I said.

Right, I knew that, he said, and looked at me. *Everything cool? You look . . . weird.*

Weird. Yeah. Exactly.

I just need a moment, I said, already questioning whether or not the bird had been real. It was so surreal I thought it *had* to be a dream or hallucination—that I had snapped awake when the leaf landed on my shoulder, just as Hub had when one landed on his nose. But I also understood that the bird being real was not the critical thing. What it had told me was: *Explore human nature and build a new wall.* And this took me back to what Yvette said just before she kissed me: *You found a way to rebuild.*

The conscious mind. The Wall of the Self. Built with the bricks we gather throughout our journey. The raw materials of life. It makes you independent, enlightened, and strong.

Protects you, too. An essential part of who we are.

I didn't have a wall. It was shattered by the wave . . . washed away.

The thing you most need is the one thing you're missing.

Ten percent of the mind . . . of the iceberg.

Rebuild.

Another leaf fell.

I'm onto something, I said to Hub.

He sat up, ears pricked, eyes wide and hopeful. *Really? Really.*

I went deeper and thought of Wayne the Fucktard—how I had gathered his hate and anger. Built a wall and buried him beneath it. I recalled how I would sometimes moan, tremble, even a curl a fist, when I took that anger for my own. What if I took more, with no intention of giving it back? And what if I flowed from place to place, person to person, and added bricks of kindness, love, sympathy, greed . . .

. . . *all of the things that you humans need.*

I'd need to use the time I had left to build a wall as strong as possible, and as high as I could reach, made up of the myriad aspects of life. Could I then do more than moan and tremble? Could I, perhaps, open my eyes at will . . . form words?

Could I walk?

Could I surf?

Could I *live*?

I'm out of here, I said to Hub.

What do you mean, he asked. *Is this . . . it?*

Hope not, I said. *But there isn't much time. I have to go to work.*

One last gnarly trick?

I need to land it, brother, I said, and couldn't resist the cheesy superhero line: *Or die trying.*

Yet another leaf spiralled down. It landed in my lap, clung to the blanket for a moment, and then fluttered away. I was about to follow it when I heard Niki's voice:

"Ohmygod." She was standing on the rear deck, pointing at me. "Mom-Dad. Come quick. Lookit!"

Had the goldfinch returned . . . maybe peck my scalp one final time, just to prove it was real? I couldn't feel it hopping around up there, so what had grabbed Niki's attention?

Oh wow, Hub said.

What's going on? I asked.

Mom, Dad, and Yvette rushed onto the deck and stared at me. Mom's face dropped in surprise and Dad ran his hands through his hair, grinning.

"That's pretty fucking far out," he said.

What is it, Hub?

The leaves, man, Hub replied, and barked excitedly. *Look at the leaves.*

I zipped from my body, joined my family on the deck, and looked.

Dad was right: pretty fucking far out.

The leaves fell behind and all around me. From that one maple. A torrent of leaves detaching from their branches and falling, flickering. Hundreds of them. They landed on my shoulders, in my lap, in my hair. Every one of them as red as the passion inside me.

"So amazing," Yvette said.

Niki pulled her cell phone from her pocket and flipped

it open to start recording, but Dad closed his hand over the device and squeezed it shut.

"No," he said. "This is our moment. It's for remembering. Not sharing."

Niki nodded, put the phone away, and they all looked at me . . . certain they were witnessing some spiritual phenomenon—that they were watching me fall from the sky.

And maybe they were.

I had other ideas, though. It was a groovy moment, no doubt . . . but all I could think about was rebuilding my wall.

All I could see falling were the leaves.

III
THE WALL

26. Our Final Moments.

Somebody somewhere is writing this down. This I know. I'm a dying (kind of), breathing genius. I'm reaching out and making it happen—from right here: the bottom of the ocean.

My name is Westlake Soul, and these are our final moments.

I ask you now . . . how would *you* spend them?

Let's take away your limitations and assume that what you experience has nothing to do with the drugs pumping through your bloodstream. You can go anywhere. Do anything. Tick off every damn thing on your bucket list. You can snowboard the Matterhorn. Sleep with the person of your dreams. Fire a gun that's bigger than you. Or perhaps you'd prefer to spend it with the people you love. Surround yourself with them and remember the good times. Feel their hands linked in yours. Their lips on your cheek.

Yeah, love beats any big gun.

Me . . . with darkness closing in?

I gave it everything I had, baby.

Release.

The world was waiting and I took to it, flying breathlessly through all its wonderment and cruelty, gathering facets of the human condition.

It's all out there . . . its God-like heartbeat. Beautiful, terrible life.

I'm going to show you so much cool stuff.

Come with me. . . .

27. ON LIFE.

I started, of course, with my family. I couldn't think of a better place to gather all the love I needed. They watched the leaves fall and I flowed through them. Yvette and Hub, too. I spread my arms and drew everything I could from their biofields. Not only love, but affection and commitment, fascination and awe. I also took what they shared with me during their goodbyes. Dad's guilt and pain. Mom's pride. Niki's aspirations. Building blocks of different shapes and sizes, but each painted by the same brush as the falling leaves. They flashed in my eyes as I stacked them. Red and gold. The colour of fire.

Do you believe in ghosts? Ever get the feeling you're not alone, or that you're being followed? How about when you catch a glimpse of something in your periphery, so fleet that you believe it imagined?

Maybe that was me, drawing from you, taking elements of your anxiety, hope, your deepest fears. A portion of every sin. A scoop of every kindness.

I went everywhere.

A church in Paris, where a woman stared at a crucifix

and whispered a prayer for the well-being of her family. Her faith was as deep and intricate as the domed ceiling, and I fluttered through it like a trapped starling. To the Italian Riviera, where an elderly man fished from a decrepit pier, and although he hadn't caught anything all day, he'd breathed the sea air and felt as young as a boy. His dark eyes sparkled with contentment, and I took all I could carry. In Bosnia and Herzegovina, a homeless man, scarred by war, sat in a grey doorway with his hand held out. I surrounded him—took tones of disheartenment and solitude. But *giving* is a part of life, too, and I dropped coins of optimism into his open hand. His fingers curled inward, as if securing something precious.

In the split seconds between destinations, I slammed these life-bricks down. Love cemented to hope and awe. Hope to fascination. Awe to despair. On and on. A wall, by God. Built broad and low to begin with—a solid foundation—but getting higher.

To a hostage in Kabul staring down the barrel of an M16. A one-year-old girl in Auckland overwhelmed by all the boxes and ribbons on her birthday. A doctor in Chennai performing surgery to save a child's sight. In Munich, a teenage boy's first kiss. And closer to home, at a cemetery in Toronto, an old man placing flowers on his wife's grave.

The sky was not big enough. I covered all of it and wanted more. I went so high that the earth appeared as small as an apple (a healthy, *ripe* apple), and I cupped it in my palm and squeezed—imagined the juices breaking through the skin and oozing between my fingers.

I went to Mathias and found Fat Annie nursing her elderly mother, wiping her forehead with a cool cloth, holding her hand. She was talking to her, the same way she used to talk to me. In a level tone, without patronizing. I wrapped myself around her and she nursed me again. Compassion. Patience. Understanding. I took it all, just as I had taken her care, then reached deep and gave her a handful of love and gratitude—let it resonate with her aura. She suddenly stopped wiping her mother's brow and turned to where I was floating, as if she could see me. Her eyes misted with tears and the most beautiful smile flowered on her face.

Thank you, Georgina, I said.

And flew away.

To a hospital in West Virginia, where emotion was stacked in crates. A woman opening her eyes for the first time—just as I had—after a crippling accident. I collected measures of her dread and consternation. Grabbed a pocketful of fear. And although I didn't have much hope to spare, I gave her some anyway. As I did with a seven-year-old girl who needed a new kidney, and a frail, frightened child with leukemia. I gave them the last of my hope—exchanged it for innocence—and felt their biofields flare. From there I went to the maternity ward and watched a newborn draw her first breath. The promise came in a thousand colours. I filled my palette and moved on.

A soldier awarded for her bravery. A scared teenager injecting heroin into his groin.

Locking those bricks together.

Higher . . . *higher*.

A helping hand offered to a stranger. A bride walking down the aisle.

It was incredible . . . inspiring. I wasn't sure if I could

rebuild my wall high enough, strong enough, but this life was, ironically, taking my breath away.

To a rundown townhouse in Hallow Falls, a green Camaro parked outside. Darryl's parents were fighting in the kitchen. As they usually were. I helped myself to a shot of their angst before floating to Darryl, who was in his bedroom clicking through photos on his Facebook page. He came to one of me and him, taken at a stag and doe four years ago. Our arms around each other. Nineteen years old and still eternal. Darryl stared at that picture for a long time, then touched the screen and said, "I could have been a better friend. All I gave you was that lousy guitar pick. I'm so sorry." Regret and sadness reverberated from him. I took a fistful of each and gave him a whisper of understanding in return. Like Fat Annie, he smiled out of nowhere, then tagged the photo and wrote in the comments section beneath: *Me and my best friend Westlake. Coolest frickin' dude EVAH!! Love you buddy!!!*

I left him smiling. Took to the skies again.

And yeah, I absorbed all the natural beauty I encountered on my journey. What better way to strengthen the wall? Time was running out, but I still circled the cones of Kilimanjaro, ran with the wildebeest across the Maasai Mara, and swam with great whites in the depths of the Indian Ocean. Nothing was taken for granted, be it a mountainside loaded with flowers or an old tree standing alone in a meadow. We are, at all times, surrounded by wonder, and I collected towering drifts of it—packed it into my wall.

My legs started to tremble. Too faintly for anyone to notice.

Something was happening. Life or death, I couldn't be sure.

I flew faster. Built stronger.

Young love in San Francisco, where—a honeybee—I drew passion from the nectar on their bodies.

Wrath at a drunken knife fight in Tijuana. Serenity in the mountains of Peru.

I heard my mother's voice. She had placed her hand on my leg and felt it trembling through the thin material of my pyjama bottoms.

"It's happening," she said, and I caught a glimpse of Niki's distraught face before pulling away.

To a clinic in Toronto, where Wayne sat with a counsellor and worked to uncover the origins of his anger. His face was pale and I saw the shadow of hurt in his eyes. "I'm afraid of being hurt," he said. "So I do the hurting. I guess it's what you call a defence mechanism, right?" I aligned with his biofield, as I had so many times before, and pulled from it not hate and anger, but insecurity and remorse. And just like that night in the alleyway, I gave something back: a glimmer of self-belief from the abundance I had collected on my journey. Enough to get him started. "I want things to be better," he said, and his broad chest expanded as he inhaled.

Running out of time. I felt my heart roaring. Gasping breaths.

My mother's hand looped around mine.

Quickly . . .

Across town, to a beautiful neo-Georgian home in Rosedale. And this didn't help my pounding heart. Not at all. But I *had* to do it.

She had grown her hair long again, and looked every bit as amazing as she had on that memorable morning—the one I go back to more often than any other, when my life branched in a cataclysmic direction, and the sunshine had been pink. This was the first time I had seen her since she walked out of my hospital room. That final glance over her shoulder, then gone forever. More than two years had passed, and though it had been tempting to ghost into her everyday life, I never had.

Until now.

Hello, Nadia, I said.

The thing with Bond girls—the ones that don't die—is that they usually end up helping Bond in some way or other. And although she would never know it, Nadia was going to help me. She didn't have to shoot any henchmen or pilot a plane away from an exploding island. All she had to do was *feel*, and I knew from personal experience that she was more than capable of doing that.

She was having a lazy day, by the look of it. Dressed—like me—in her pyjamas, snacking on a bowl of chips, watching *MTV Cribs* on a TV the size of some of the homes I'd visited in South America. I floated beside her, wondering what her life had been like in the last two years, and it was only when I swirled my hands through her aura that I realized she was pregnant. I drew back, a little surprised, but happy for her, even though I couldn't see a ring on her finger. That didn't matter, of course, but I thought it probably mattered to Nadia. *I want to be your Soul*, she had said to me, and I remembered the dream she had picked out for us: Marvel and Calypso, and our garden made of sand.

Nadia wanted it all. She always had.

I flowed through her and found shades of anxiety and excitement. I took a small portion of each for my wall—I had to have Nadia in my wall; she was such a big part of my life—and gave her a generous cut of assurance. Forgiveness, too, and no small amount of love. She sat upright on the sofa, the chips spilling from her lap, one hand clutching her breast. I imagined the memories crashing through her mind. The same ones that had crashed through mine, over and over again.

I can't tell the future, I said to her. *Not one of my amazing superhero abilities. But I have a feeling you're going to be just fine. Both of you.*

Time . . . ticking surely away, but I couldn't resist a curious ex-boyfriend moment. I drifted up to her bedroom and looked for evidence of the father—the man who may yet put a ring on her finger. Maybe a photo on the nightstand. Nadia cheek-to-cheek with some dude who looked like Matthew McConaughey. Or even, if I was lucky, her Facebook open—soppy messages and countless emoticons decorating her wall (a different kind of wall, but still a symbol of her life), along with pictures of the blissful couple at family gatherings or on some trendy rooftop bar. Yeah, I was curious, you're damn right. And maybe hurting a little, if I'm being honest. But I mainly wanted to make sure that the dude checked out . . . that he looked cool.

I found nothing, though. Her bedroom looked hauntingly similar to how it had when I'd been dating her. Same pale green walls. Same furniture.

Are you alone, Nadia?

If she was now, I knew she wouldn't be for long. The

men might come and go, but in about six months she'd have someone she could love forever, and spend the rest of her life with.

And she would be their soul.

An open notebook on her desk caught my attention. I ghosted over to it and saw that Nadia had half-filled one of the pages with her loveable, looping script. She'd written BABY NAMES along the top, underlined with three wavy lines. Beneath this: GIRL on the left side, BOY on the right. The list of girls' names stretched to the bottom of the page. Madelyn, Zoey, Amy, Chiara . . . But there was only one name in the running for a boy:

Westlake.

I smiled . . . started to drift away. *Hey*, I thought. *Maybe he'll grow up to be one of Gladys Knight's Pips*. And I was just about to move on—I had one last thing to do—when I was stopped solid by a sound from downstairs. Instantly chilling, yet undeniably beautiful. I thought my ethereal presence would turn to ice, fall heavily from the air, and shatter into so many pieces.

She was playing it again . . . Beethoven's *Sonata pathétique*.

Our song.

I went from being able to span the world in half a second, to having no control whatsoever. I was lifted, twirled around, swept downward, turned upside down. Like that feather at the beginning of *Forrest Gump*. Before I knew it, I was swaying into the music room, with its funky artwork and rich lavender smell. Nadia sat at the Steinway in her Hello Kitty pyjamas, her fingers barely touching the keys, yet evoking such inspiring sound. A blend of subtlety and power that filled the room with life. I drifted above the raised lid and looked at her. Delicate and composed. Elegance soaring from her. And again, the music overwhelmed me. The creation of heat. Nuclear fusion. It had formed a miniature sun before, but now it was helping to form my wall.

I took every note—every beat of passion—and gave back a wave of good feeling.

The ultimate SuperPoke.

Her breast and shoulders trembled, but her fingers didn't falter. She turned her wet eyes to where I floated above the piano, and I saw her smile for the first time since that morning in Tofino.

I reached for her—my fingers, so lightly, outlining her body, but still not as lightly as she touched those keys.

Thank you, I said. Not exactly a Bond-style one-liner, but it was all I had. All I needed. Nadia responded by playing the final note, and before it had faded from the lavender-scented air, I was gone.

Back home, my family had brushed the leaves from my hair and shoulders and moved me back into the groovy room. They were gathered around my bed, even Hub, who looked on anxiously. My eyes were closed and my chest heaved as I laboured for each breath. Niki was hugging Dad, both of them in tears. Mom held my hand and waited.

"Okay, baby," she said. "We love you so much. It's okay."

"Look at him shaking," Niki said. "It was supposed to be peaceful. You said he wouldn't feel anything."

Dad held her and said nothing. Mom squeezed my hand harder.

"Okay, baby . . . okay."

I left their grief and pain behind and went searching for the final piece of my wall—the one thing I had refused to embrace, and an essential part of all life.

It was easy to find. I knew it would be.

He had been waiting for me all along.

I'm here, I said, feeling the sand between my toes, the stale air rushing over my naked skin. *I'm not running anymore.*

He comes in all forms. I have seen him as small as a spider, and as large as a mountain. With wings, and without. Breathing fire, and wrapped in ice. Sometimes he is seductive, and sometimes cruel.

But now, for the first time, I was looking at his true face.

And it was perfect.

Hello, old friend, Dr. Quietus roared. His mouth crashed and foamed.

I pulled my shoulders square, grabbed my board, and stepped toward the ocean.

28. On Death.

I remember the first time I went surfing. Fourteen years old. Cocoa Beach, Florida. We'd been on vacation, had spent some time at Grandma Soul's commune before taking a week at the beach. Being fourteen, I was given something of a free rein (provided I stayed within sight of our apartment), so figured I'd go down to the beach and check out the honeys—their tanned bodies peppered with sand, bikinis riding up the cracks of their asses. I spent more time watching the surfers, though. Bringing the waves in, landing aerials. Then jamming the tails of their boards in the sand and hanging in packs on the beach, chilling out and swapping stories. I loved the image, too. Sun-bleached hair and toned bodies, rope necklaces, baggy shorts, or wetsuits that they'd roll down to their waists when they weren't in the breaks.

I decided . . . that was the life for me.

I persuaded Dad to buy me a board. "Where the hell are you going to surf back in Canada?" he asked. A reasonable argument, but I would not be swayed. He got me a 6'6" thruster from Ron Jon's. Not much, but I loved that board, man—think I rode more waves on that than any other. Wiped out on more, too. I used my allowance to buy the essential accessories: a decent leash, a shoulder bag, a block of Mr. Zog's Sex Wax, and a rope necklace, of course. I went down to the beach—shaking off Dad's offer to come with—but I was too afraid to go in the water. I thrust the tail of my board in the sand and sat in the wedge of its shadow, watching everybody else. That was as close as I got to being a surfer that day.

The following day, though, I moved a little closer to the action, and eventually got talking to an older surfer named Vix. A real cool dude—looked like Jeff Bridges in *The Big Lebowski.* He looked at my board and asked why I wasn't getting it wet, and I told him that I didn't know where to begin. Dude gave me a few pointers from the safety of dry land: how to wax my board, popping up techniques, where to place my feet. Then I took to the water for the first time. I managed to body-surf several waves and—kook that I was—break a few rules of surfing etiquette, but try as I might, I couldn't pop up. Couldn't spring to my feet and stay there. I'd get to one knee and—*whoosh*—wipeout, baby. It got later. The sun painted a tangerine stripe across the western sky. The tide rolled in. Most of the surfers had packed up, went off to shower and eat and party. But I kept trying . . . trying. Eventually, with a rash on my chest and my whole body aching, I gave up. Slumped out of the water with my head low and threw my board into the sand.

"That ain't no way to treat a stick, man," a voice to my left said. Made me jump, too. I snapped in that direction and saw Vix sitting on the fringe of the beach, all but hidden in the sea grass swaying behind him. He looked at me and smiled. His crinkled eyes caught the setting sun, as bright as new pennies.

"Surfing sucks," I said to him.

"Are you kidding me, man?" he said. "When you get up on a wave . . . man, feels like you'll live forever."

"But I can't get up," I groaned. "Been trying all day, and my arms are killing me."

Vix smiled wider and shrugged. "Well, one thing I know . . . you'll never get up if you quit." He looked at the ocean, his eyes on fire. "It's like learning to walk, man. First time you try, you fall on your ass. Second and third time, too. Then eventually you get up, and you *stay* up. And that's not just walking, man, or surfing. That's *life*. The whole goddamn ride."

"I guess," I said.

"Yeah, you guess," he said. "Pick up that stick, man, and come back tomorrow. If you can get to your feet and stay there as a baby, you can for damn sure do it as a young man."

I nodded, picked up my board.

"You can't be afraid, man." Vix said, and looked at me. "Not if you want to be alive."

So I went back the following morning. Vix wasn't there, but the ocean was. Like it always has been, and always will be. I put my board in the water and within a few sets, I was on my feet—a little wobbly, for sure, but on my feet.

And alive.

So alive.

You fall on your ass. You get up . . . and eventually you stay up.

I haven't backed down from a wave, or a challenge, since.

Surf's up, superhero, Dr. Quietus said. *Show me what you've got.*

It wasn't your beach in paradise, I can tell you. The sea was so dark, and the sand so pale, that it looked like I had fallen into one of those nightmarish art house movies shot entirely in black and white. *Eraserhead Goes Surfing*, perhaps. The sun was a blanched eye boiling in a sky the colour of burned chrome, and the air smelled not of salt and seaweed, but of decay and smoke. At least the beach was sandy (littered with small bones, but sandy), although off to both sides I saw spikes of rock, like giant broken bottles. Easy to imagine the ocean taking me, smashing my body into them, ending me forever.

Definitely not paradise.

He spoke with the ocean's voice, heard in every crashing wave: *This is it, Westlake Soul.* Cresting, breaking hard, and spitting cold spray. *This is the end.*

Khalil Gibran, the noted Lebanese poet, wrote, "You would know the secret of Death. But how shall you find it unless you seek it in the heart of life?" Vix had told me the same thing, although less poetically: *You can't be afraid, man. Not if you want to be alive.* I had, since my accident, resisted death . . . run away. Better to turn my face. To hide. But the secret of death—or any inevitability—is to not be afraid of it. Nothing is accomplished through fear. Once tamed, anything is possible. *Anything.* That's not only the secret of death, brothers and sisters . . . it's the secret of life, too.

The whole goddamn ride.

I stepped closer to the water. Felt the wind skimming off the backs of waves.

That's it, the ocean said. *Come to me.*

No one else on the beach. No one to save me this time. I was on my own.

Come . . .

I nodded and my hair blew across my face and the ocean was black and wild but I wasn't afraid. I kept walking, my board tucked under my arm. My first board, of course—the thruster from Ron Jon's that I had learned on.

This is it . . .

I stepped into the water. Cold surf bubbled around my ankles. There was no need to read the breaks; it was all heavy, and I wasn't backing down, anyway. I pushed off and paddled out to deeper water, body-surfed the first few waves to gauge speed and power. My board shook beneath me and I gripped the rails hard. The ocean boomed and I saw shapes in the surf. They looked like pale hands, drowned faces.

I'm ready for this, I said.

Dr. Quietus laughed. He raised his black arms and brought them down hard.

It was like the horizon hunched its shoulders. From left to right, as far as I could see, a growing ridge of water, rolling toward me.

Here I come, Westlake Soul.

Swelling, filling the sky.

You don't stand a chance.

This was the wave—the end. One way or another. I was either getting the better of it, or I'd be cremated with Angus Young's guitar pick by the end of the week.

It came at me like spread wings. Unthinkable span. I faced the beach and started to paddle, trying to get up enough speed to glide into the wave. My stiff arms ached but I didn't stop. Worked harder when I felt the wave behind me. It sounded like war. Grenades exploding. Guns firing. Missiles hitting their targets. I heard screaming, too. There was a mile of water beneath me and it was packed—I was *sure* of it—with screaming bodies. I paddled harder and felt the push behind the board. The power was incredible but I managed to pop to my feet in one fluid motion. I carved the face and dropped down, hard as a block of granite. The board kicked beneath me and I came close to losing it, but shifted my weight at the critical moment and maintained balance.

Cold spray in my face, biting my skin. It stung my eyes, tasted like sulphur.

Dr. Quietus roared and reached for me with thick, dark arms. I caught a burst of speed and almost lost it again, but drove into the flats to hit my bottom turn. I ascended the wave and, with growing confidence, launched into an aerial. I soared, twisting three-sixty through midair—weightless, like I'd hit orbit—and saw the wave falling beneath me.

Falling . . .

But I was flying. Breathlessly high and with a booming heart.

One last gnarly trick.

I looked down and saw that the ridge of the wave had become the top of a wall. *My* wall. Rebuilt. Towering and powerful.

I grabbed my board and flew over it—came down on the face of a different wave.

Cool and blue.

A different ocean.

29. Down.

I spilled from my board, hit the water and went deep.
Could've kicked to the surface, but I enjoyed the feel of the
ocean around me too much. So cool. So alive. It streamed
into my hair. Into my eyes and mouth. Around my muscles.

It felt like being held.

I went deeper, through schools of fish like mirror
shards, and pods of singing humpbacks. Down, into a layer
of darkness, and beyond . . . where lobates flowed around
me like natural satellites, and were dragged deeper by my
diving mass.

30. And Out.

My name is Westlake Soul, and these are our final moments.

Westlake . . . baby . . .

Bottom of the ocean. Darkness all around, but a whisper of light above. Like a window that has been painted black, all but the thinnest crack. And I can see out, at the sky, perhaps. Surf City Blue.

I should swim closer . . . take a look.

Open my eyes.

Soon.

For now, though, I like how the current rocks me from side to side. It feels so different. *Cool*, for one thing. Comforting, too. I know that if I project from my body—with the last of my superhero power—I will see Mom holding me. She will be stroking my face with one hand. The other will be curled into mine. Tears falling. Salt water on my lips.

Baby . . .

I'll feel her love—a breathtaking miniature sun—and remember what she asked me when the ocean was cold and dark.

WESTLAKE SOUL

What do you want, Westlake?
I will surface. Grab her hand and squeeze firmly.
"More," I will say, and open my eyes.

ACKNOWLEDGEMENTS

You don't write a novel like *Westlake Soul* without a little help and love en route. Not if you want it to be worth reading, at least. I owe so much to the following people, who gave me their help, or love (and in some cases both), and without whom this novel would have been very different . . . and certainly not sitting in your hands.

The Ontario Arts Council, for their generous support and continued good work; Claude Lalumière, for his help with the French translations (many humorous e-mails were exchanged, believe me); Mark Morris and Joel A. Sutherland, my wonderful beta readers, who offered excellent suggestions and proved themselves as essential as I knew they would be; the three doctors (in no particular order): Dr. Tressa Amirthanayagam, who cast her expert eye over an early draft, and whose enthusiasm buoyed the numerous revisions; Dr. Andrew Marsh (a real life super genius), who patiently provided information on such topics as bioresonant energy and quantum entanglement, and in a way that I (not a super genius) could grasp; Dr. Paul Hosek, who does fantastic work with PVS patients every day, and who proved invaluable—as a doctor and a reader—in ways I can't even begin to describe.

And where would *Westlake* be without the inimitable CZP gang? Samantha Beiko, Helen Marshall, Laura Marshall, Matt Moore, Danny Evarts. Thank you so much. And yes, dammit, I love you all. Erik Mohr, cover artist extraordinaire, and the reason this book looks so damn pretty. Sandra Kasturi, who believed in *Westlake* from the very beginning. Her faith and support has been nothing short of breathtaking. And, of course, my editor at CZP, Brett Savory, to whom I pitched *Westlake Soul* as we drunkenly staggered through the hallways of a hotel somewhere in the GTA. He didn't ridicule my idea too much (although I could see the glaze of uncertainty in his eyes), and so I brought *Westlake* to life. And look at us now, brotherman. Look at us now. . . .

Finally . . . my beautiful wife, Emily. My superhero. The sun in miniature. For too many reasons to mention. Suffice to say that some aspects of this novel were difficult to write, and some were not.

Everything about love, for instance . . . all too easy, because of her.

ABOUT THE AUTHOR

Rio Youers has been praised by some of the most noteworthy names in the speculative fiction genre. He is the British Fantasy Award-nominated author of *Old Man Scratch* and *End Times*. His short fiction has been published by, among others, Edge Science Fiction & Fantasy, IDW, and PS Publishing. Rio lives in southwestern Ontario with his wife, Emily, and their daughter, Lily Maye.

SHOEBOX TRAIN WRECK

JOHN MANTOOTH

AVAILABLE MARCH 2012
FROM CHIZINE PUBLICATIONS

978-1-926851-54-9

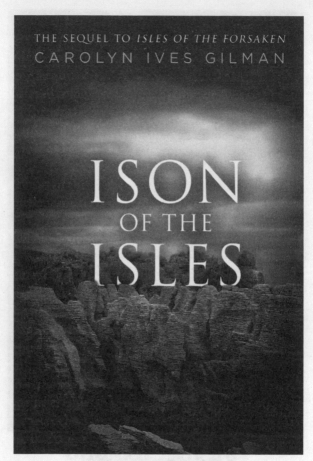

ISON OF THE ISLES

CAROLYN IVES GILMAN

AVAILABLE APRIL 2012
FROM CHIZINE PUBLICATIONS

978-1-926851-56-3

A TREE OF BONES

VOLUME THREE OF THE HEXSLINGER SERIES
GEMMA FILES

AVAILABLE MAY 2012
FROM CHIZINE PUBLICATIONS

978-1-926851-57-0

NINJA VERSUS PIRATE
FEATURING ZOMBIES

JAMES MARSHALL

AVAILABLE MAY 2012
FROM CHIZINE PUBLICATIONS

978-1-926851-58-7

RASPUTIN'S BASTARDS

DAVID NICKLE

AVAILABLE JUNE 2012
FROM CHIZINE PUBLICATIONS

978-1-926851-59-4

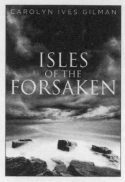

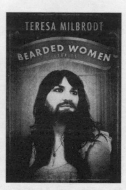
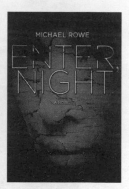

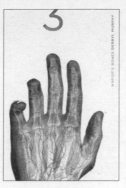

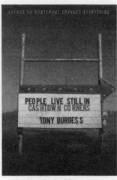